IN THE DOODOO
WITH VOODOO

STEVE HIGGS

VINCI
BOOKS

Vinci Books

vinci-books.com

Published by Vinci Books Ltd in 2025

1

A CIP catalogue record for this book is available from the British Library.
Paperback ISBN: 9781036708566

The EU GPSR authorised representative is Logos Europe, 9 rue Nicolas Poussion, 17000 La Rochelle, France contact@logoseurope.eu

By Steve Higgs

Blue Moon Investigations

Paranormal Nonsense

The Phantom of Barker Mill

Amanda Harper Paranormal Detective

The Klowns of Kent

Dead Pirates of Cawsand

In the Doodoo with Voodoo

The Witches of East Malling

Crop Circles, Cows and Crazy Aliens

Whispers in the Rigging

Paws of the Yeti

Under a Blue Moon

Night Work

Lord Hale's Monster

Herne Bay Howlers

Undead Incorporated

The Ghoul of Christmas Past

The Sandman

Jailhouse Golem

Sparks in the Darkness

Shadow in the Mine

Ghost Writer

Monsters Everywhere

Modern Fairy Tale
No Such Thing as Magic

Albert Smith Culinary Capers

Pork Pie Pandemonium
Bakewell Tart Bludgeoning
Stilton Slaughter
Bedfordshire Clanger Calamity
Death of a Yorkshire Pudding
Cumberland Sausage Shocker
Arbroath Smokie Slaying
Dundee Cake Deception
Lancashire Hotpot Peril
Blackpool Rock Bloodshed
Kent Coast Oyster Obliteration
Eton Mess Massacre
Cornish Pasty Conspiracy
The Gastrothief
Lyme Regis Layover
Majestic Mystery

Last Shift

I hate running. I was sure I shouldn't have to run this much as a police officer. Surely, when I shout for a criminal to stop running, they should stop. This guy hadn't read the rules though, so he was tearing down Week Street in Maidstone with no intention of slowing down.

He was just a petty pickpocket, one of a gang that had been targeting Maidstone town centre recently, snatching purses and pilfering wallets. Or lifting people's shopping bags when they weren't looking. There was always a crime being committed in Maidstone town centre, it was just that kind of town where people with money mixed with those who did not, and certain parties tried to even the balance.

I was posted in plain clothes to observe and ultimately find the gang. Basically, I' been sent window shopping for the day with a side order of try to pay attention to what's going on around you. It was my very last shift with the police.

I quit several weeks ago when I finally admitted that my career wasn't going anywhere. It coincided with meeting

Tempest Michaels, a local, self-employed paranormal investigator. I asked him for a job, and he signed me up right then and there. Now I work for him, but I still have a week of notice left in my old job, so I was kinda working both simultaneously.

Sipping a salted caramel hot chocolate and telling myself that ordering it skinny meant it was really low in calories, I was paying almost no attention to anything, when right in front of me the dopey looking kid with the spots and the dreadlocks walked up to a pram, opened a lady's handbag, and pulled out her purse. He even looked up at me as he slid it into the pocket of his dirty hoody and had the audacity to wink.

I thought he was going to try me with a chat up line until I yanked out my warrant card and shouted for him to stop.

He didn't of course. Which was how I came to now be chasing the ugly, skinny little turd down Week Street towards the river. He was faster than me, but he also wore his jeans hood style, so they were flapping around his backside and threatening to fall down and trip him the whole time. He probably thought they looked cool.

I yelled into my microphone that I was chasing a suspect and needed back up in position. There were three of us working undercover today in different parts of the town centre, but it's so big that we couldn't easily coordinate between us. Uniformed police are also never far away in Maidstone though and today two were positioned at the top of Fremlin Walk where the confluence of roads creates a hub of sorts.

The youth ran by them almost before I could react, certainly before I could raise a warning to anyone, so my backup was essentially backing me up now by running along behind me.

Not much help.

A cyclist came out of the cut through by Earl's pub, almost knocking the kid with the dreadlocks over. He leaped over his front wheel though as the cyclist saw him at the last moment and hit his brakes. The move put the cyclist directly in my path and I ploughed right into him, the pair of us going down to slam into the ground. Me on top of him with his surprised face jammed between my boobs.

The guys in uniform leapt over the tangle of bike, cyclist, and me to continue the pursuit, but the pickpocket had gained valuable yards. Despite that, the likelihood of him escaping remained slim. Maidstone is too open. There are no clever alleyways to duck down to aid his evasion. His only hope was to pick up a bike or get into a car.

No sooner had the thought left my brain, than a brand-new white Mercedes C220i AMG flew out of the gap by the Hazlitt Theatre. Someone inside threw the passenger's door open, and it skidded to a halt. The youth was going to make it. He had too great a lead to be caught now.

Until Patience clotheslined him.

I didn't even see where she came from. I was still picking myself up and making sure my boobs weren't hanging out of my top. One second, he was home free, the next his body was spinning through the air while his head rotated about Patience's right forearm.

Score one for the girls!

Patience is one of the other officers placed in town to look for the pickpocket gang. We had been sent to different areas of the town to cover the most amount of territory, but she'd been messaging me since we arrived to meet up and

3

work together because she was bored and wanted to quiz me about my boyfriend.

I apologised to the poor cyclist and got moving again.

Seeing his accomplice get taken down, the driver of the Mercedes hit the gas and belted down Week Street towards the A229 where he could filter into the freely moving Sunday traffic and escape. He wasn't having a good day, though.

Ahead of him, the lights changed, and an Argos truck swept out of Pudding Lane. With nowhere to go, I watched the brake lights flash accompanied by the screeching of tyres before he slammed nose first into the side of the truck, ruining the beautiful new German car. To be fair, it was probably stolen.

Patience stood over the thief. I was out of breath, but there was no longer any cause to hurry, so I ambled towards her at a fast walk. Downhill from me, Duncan and Sylvester, the two chaps in uniform, caught up to the ailing car just as the driver tried to bail out. In moments, was cuffed and forced into a sitting position by the car's rear wheel.

'Hey, butt monkey!' Patience was making her arrest. The youth was lying on the pavement groaning a little and slowly writhing around in pain. 'Hey! I'm arresting you for the crime of having a ridiculous haircut, terrible clothes and for being a dirty little purse snatcher.' Patience didn't worry too much about doing her job properly so long as she enjoyed herself.

I arrived at her position where a small crowd was beginning to gather. Human nature dictates shoppers or passersby are always ready for a little street theatre.

'Hey, girl.' She offered me a high five. 'Did you see the sale on at House of Fraser? I nearly spent next month's wages. They have too much fine clothing.'

Thinking what we needed to do was our jobs, I said, 'We should get this one to the station.'

'The uniforms can pick him up in a minute. Patience needs some lunch.' She was staring at my chest. 'You know your boobs are lopsided right?'

I looked down. Dressing this morning for undercover work in town, it hadn't occurred to me to put on a sports bra. I wasn't expecting to chase anyone. I turned away from her to rearrange myself, then realised I had a three-hundred and sixty-degree crowd. My boobs were going to have to wait.

A squad car made its way past the wreckage at the bottom of the road, being waved on by Sylvester. A second car was behind it and behind that a third car which would probably contain Chief Inspector Quinn. The second car peeled off to stay with the crashed Mercedes, so I groaned internally as CI Quinn's car kept on coming.

Both cars ground to a halt right next to us, the crowd parting only when Patience yelled at them to do so.

Three uniformed constables exited the cars, the driver of CI Quinn's car opening the rear door to let him out. He's pompous and pretentious and doesn't realise that having people to open doors for him demonstrates that more clearly than anything else could.

Regardless, he was heading to the top of the ladder and acting as if he ought to be there already worked for him. He and I had an unsteady relationship that went back about six years to when he was my sergeant, and I spurned his advances.

In a few days, it would no longer be of any concern. I didn't hand my ID card back officially until November 8th, but due to overtime coupled with vacation days I never got around to taking, I was finishing today. My uniform and all the paraphernalia that went with it was in the boot of my car ready to be handed back. I had hoped I could wrap the undercover thing up quickly enough to get back to the station and hand it all in, but alas it was already too late for that, so I would have to return tomorrow or the day after.

'Woods, report,' Quinn demanded.

'Got us an ugly idiot with a head full of dreadlocks, Chief. Woman's purse still in his possession. I think he looks like he might try to run again. You want me to kick him in the bollocks?'

The guys in uniform snorted laughter they tried hard to control.

'Woods, you know how I enjoy your reports. Please stick to the facts and try not to embarrass yourself perpetually?' CI Quinn replied deadpan. He's not known for his sense of humour.

'Was that a yes or a no on the bollocks?' she enquired, seeming genuinely unsure. 'A no, then.' She decided, seeing his expression.

I was getting peckish. I had managed one small swig of my hot chocolate before I had to abandon it to chase Mr Dreadlocks, so now I was both hungry and thirsty and it was getting close to lunchtime.

'Do you need anything further from us here, sir?' I asked CI Quinn directly. 'Perhaps Patience and I should return to observing the crowd in case there are more of his gang operating here?'

Ben Swanscombe cuffed the youth and got him to his feet.

'She hit me,' the boy protested. 'She's not allowed to hit me.'

'I stopped you is what I did. You ran into me. I was stationary, and you were moving. You can't claim I hit you if

I didn't move.' Patience was well used to defending her slightly violent streak.

The youth continued to complain as he was led away and bundled into the back of the squad car.

CI Quinn turned to leave, but over his shoulder, he said, 'I want you both back at the station. You have paperwork to fill out.' He ducked into his car, either to ensure we couldn't reply or probably because he's so disinterested in anything we might have to say that he'd already forgotten us.

'Well, Patience is going for lunch, Chief Inspector. What do you think about that?' she said to the departing car. 'Damn that white boy sure has a stick in his butt. What do you want for lunch girl? Patience is buying?'

'You're buying? You win the lottery or something?' I'm not saying Patience is tight with her money, I just don't remember her ever having any.

'Girl, it's your last day. Or at least it's your last shift. Patience is going to buy you lunch.' Patience was displaying one of her rare moments of seriousness. She's a good friend. The kind I suspected I could rely on if I ever needed to. We had already promised to stay in touch even though we would no longer be working together every week.

'Lunch sounds good,' I replied. It really did.

'And a large glass of pinot,' she added.

'We're still on duty. We're not allowed to drink.'

'Girl, it's your last day. When are you ever going to break the rules if not now? What are they going to do if they catch you?'

She had a point. 'Okay, Patience. A glass of pinot.'

'Large glass.'

'Large glass,' I conceded.

'And shots.'

A New Case

Lunch with Patience had not been a good idea. It seemed like one at the time, especially when the first half glass of cool, crisp, perfect white wine wound its sensuous tendrils of relaxation into me and removed the stress I was feeling. After that took hold, I remember deciding that another glass was a great idea and my planned lunchtime skinny salad had been abandoned in favour of a pizza. Then a third glass had happened and the two of us had slunk back to the Station three hours later, armed with a quickly concocted lie about having seen some probable pickpockets and feeling the need to tail them.

No one asked us where we had been though, as if they hadn't even noticed we were absent. I finished my paperwork, writing up a report about the event in town, the chase, and arrest, while next to me Patience worked her way through several doughnuts she'd picked up on the way back to the station because all the wine had made her hungry.

Whether I was stressed because it was my last day with a steady sensible job and the pay check for it was about to run out, or if I was worried about my new career as a paranormal investigator, I hadn't been introspective enough to work out. When I talked to Patience about it, somewhere between glass two and glass three, she said it was neither thing. In her opinion, I was getting stressed because I knew I was going to have to sleep with my perfect boyfriend soon and now I was worried that she had it right.

I had met Brett Barker about a day after I took the job at the Blue Moon Investigation Agency. He was a prime suspect in the murder of his grandfather, not least because he'd inherited the Barker Steel Mill in Dartford and a sizeable fortune upon the man's death. Tempest Michaels, that's the owner of the Blue Moon business and my boss, thought Brett was guilty, and all the evidence suggested he was. I had arrested him, as I was still a serving police officer, but released him the next day when we determined he was innocent, and he asked me on a date.

That was two weeks ago, and we had been on several dates since. I'm counting him as my boyfriend already, but we haven't yet managed to get to the intimate part of our relationship. Honestly, I don't know why we haven't. There has not been a conversation where we have decided to take it slow. I'm certain he's not gay, and we are both old enough to not be tiptoeing around, yet nothing beyond some passionate kissing has occurred thus far.

Patience assures me that if I don't take him to bed soon, I will lose him. Actually, that wasn't what Patience said. She said ... never mind. Let's just say it was a more graphic version of hurry up and take him to bed.

And it was what I was planning to do. He was gorgeous. He was lean and athletic with a handsome face that smiled easily. He's an absolute gentleman and he is seriously rich. Like, buy me an island for my birthday kind of rich. We were taking it in turns to entertain each other. One date he would call the shots and take me out. Sometimes it had been swanky and expensive, like the first date when he put me on a commercial jet flying first class to Paris for an overnight stay at the Penthouse of the Ritz, but he'd also taken me out for dinner in a perfectly ordinary restaurant.

That we earned vastly different amounts was of no concern to him it seemed, it would only be a concern in our relationship at all if I decided it was, so I had to get over it. When it had been my turn to entertain him, I had brought him to my house for pizza, or out to the local cinema because there was a film I wanted to see. Five dates had elapsed now though. Was that too many without some intimacy creeping in?

I had answered the question for myself days ago but had done nothing about it yet. Now it was time to fix the problem before it became one. I would call him tonight, invite him to my flat tomorrow night and shag his beautiful brains out.

The clock on the wall assured me it was nearly finishing time for me. I would have to return in a couple of days to hand back my uniform and again on November 8th to hand over my ID card. I felt no pang of separation at the thought of being without that vital piece of equipment. It was just something I had carried around with me for the last few years.

Just as I was getting out of my chair to leave, my phone rang. The caller ID on the screen told me it was Jane/James calling. Jane/James is Tempest's cross-dressing, gender fluid office assistant. A young man who with a wig, some makeup and a dress, looks more convincing as a woman than I do.

'Amanda Harper,' I answered the phone.

'Hi, Amanda. It's James,' he said. 'Are you coming to work tomorrow? We have a couple of promising cases.'

'I will be there. Just one question: Where is there now?' Two days ago, the Blue Moon office had been subjected to a firebomb and had burned to the ground. It would be rebuilt, but for now, it was very much unusable.

'Tempest has set me up in the office in his house. It feels a bit odd wandering around his house without him here, but at least we are still in business.'

'Tempest isn't there? Where is he?' I asked.

'I'll tell you about it in the morning. Or Tempest will call you I guess,' he replied.

That was cryptic. I dismissed it though. Tempest would come and go in pursuit of cases as he saw fit. He wasn't there to hold my hand and had hired me because of my ability to work independently. The pair of us might work together on cases at times but would just as often attend to separate clients.

'What are the cases?' I asked him.

'There are a few actually. The Tonbridge ghost tours are once again claiming to have a ghost that they want us to investigate, there are some farmers out towards Cliffe that have reported mysterious crop circles coupled with odd behaviour from their cattle. However, the most pressing seems to be from a young lady that has become the target of a voodoo priest.'

'Voodoo?'

'Yes.'

'In Kent?'

'Apparently so. She met some guy on a dating website. He got a little scary and when she broke it off, he cursed her, and her hair has fallen out.'

I had picked my phone up, air-kissed Patience and

headed out the door. I had to leave my car in the space behind the station as I wasn't at all certain I was sober enough to drive home. Fortunately, it was only a little more than a mile to my flat by the train station. I was still talking when I got outside and discovered it had started to drizzle.

Nuts.

'Are you still there, Amanda?' James asked.

'Yes, still here. Just fighting with my umbrella.' I needed both hands. 'James, I will see you at Tempest's house at nine o'clock tomorrow. Okay?'

'Sure thing.'

'I expect the cases can wait until then.' I said goodbye and disconnected. The damned umbrella catch was sticking and refusing to open. I was hovering in the doorway at the back of the station grunting and swearing. Finally, it popped, and the handbag-handy brolly flung itself from closed to inside out and then mockingly refused to go back to a useable state. It learned to rue the day as I shoved its useless arse into the first trash bin I came to.

I trudged home through the increasing downpour, my hair a sodden mess on my shoulders by the time I got there. Mrs Stone was just wheeling her bin outside when I came hurrying up the path towards our building. I lived in a four-story block of flats not far from Maidstone East train station. The location was favoured by city commuters heading to London as the price of living here was far more affordable than the cost of living inside a London postcode. I was fortunate enough to have secured a flat on the top floor when they were first built five years ago. It was a small place but was still easily big enough for me and had been fitted out with good quality cupboards and appliances in the kitchen and was also well-appointed in the bathroom. The rent was affordable – more so now that I was going to earn more with the switch in jobs and I saw no reason to move. A small, but insistent voice at the back of my head, that sounded suspiciously like my mother, told me I should marry Brett and move into his twenty-five-bedroom palace.

I ignored it.

I hadn't actually been to Brett's house yet as a girlfriend. The last time I was there I was tossing the place looking for evidence. I would get there soon enough but I was in no hurry to be a wife, or a mother or anything other than what I was. Mostly I struggled to look after myself, all too often discovered that I had no clean knickers to put on and regularly opened the fridge to find there was no food in it. Each time I did so I promised to organise myself better. But I never did.

'Hi, Mrs Stone,' I called out in passing. She was wearing a pink warm-up suit and pink sparkly fake Ugg boots. Her silver hair was also dyed a shade of pink and to contrast it all, she had on a terry dressing gown in a lemon hue.

She waved a hand in reply as she manoeuvred her bin into place by the kerb ready for the morning. I made a note that I needed to do the same as they only came every other week and I had missed the last two collections.

Pushing open my door, I stepped over the mail I found on the floor inside, then scooped it up and quickly sifted it on my way through to the kitchen area. Mostly rubbish I concluded but there was one envelope that looked suspiciously like my credit card bill, I left that one for later, and a postcard from my Mum. I dumped everything but the postcard on the kitchen counter along with my handbag as I continued through to the bathroom where I set the bath taps to run hot water. My hair was already wet, so a bath seemed perfectly timed. I swiped my phone to connect to the speaker and pressed play. A heavy base started thumping through my apartment as I sashayed into the bedroom to peel off my damp clothes.

I put the postcard face down on my dressing table, so I could read it as I fumbled with my clothes. My mother and her boyfriend, Max were on a round-the-world cruise. Mum had retired earlier this year when Max had convinced her she should. Dad had died six years ago when his battle with cancer was finally done, and I thought mum would never smile again. Then last year, about eighteen months ago now, she met Max at a friend's sixtieth birthday party. He was a few years younger than her but pointed out that at their age it didn't make all that much difference.

I was happy for her, but her relationship with Max came with one unfortunate side effect – her renewed sex life. I had learned, not that I wanted to, that my mother had married the first man she slept with. A fact she only came to regret after he'd died, and she found out what she'd been missing. Now she was, so far as I could tell, only sleeping with the second man ever, but he was more experienced or more adventurous or more something and she wanted to tell me about it every time we sat down to chat.

Thankfully, there was no mention of sex in the note she sent me. They were now on the final leg and having passed through the Panama Canal were in Miami. It would be another couple of weeks before they were home although, of course, the postcard took a while to get to me even in the 21st century and mum liked to send them rather than emails that would be instantly delivered. She was having the time of her life, and I was happy for her.

Now naked and getting cool, I hurried to the bathroom and slipped into the tub. I had expected to feel buoyant this evening. I need never put my uniform on again. I ought to be celebrating. Oddly though, I felt a little uncomfortable, as if I had done something wrong and was about to be exposed for it.

My phone rang. It wasn't a number I recognised so I Ignored it, let it ring off and I flicked the button to silent as I slipped into the bath. Ordinarily, I would have taken a glass of wine with me, but after the overindulgence this afternoon I was sipping water instead.

Forty-five minutes of soaking, scrubbing, exfoliating and moisturising later I was getting hungry. The pizza, eaten in a wine induced haze of false hunger was now forgotten, demanding I forage for sustenance again very soon.

First though, I would call Brett. It was a call I had been planning in my head for a couple of days. I wanted to get him naked, and I wanted him to know that this was my plan, but in a subtle, sexy way that would leave him hopeful, but not certain of my intentions.

I really ought not to feel nervous. I found it both exhilarating and worrying that I did. Brett Barker was very much unlike any other man I had ever met. Ignoring the bank account that equalled a small European Country's GDP, he was a man that was at the same time utterly confident and yet still somehow unsure of himself. That he could nurture in me a desire to look after him while also willingly giving myself up as his sex-slave gave me a rush. He was exquisitely handsome, and I could only imagine what he would look like naked. On the few occasions when my hands had touched his arms, or torso or anything else, it was clear he was lean and muscular beneath his clothing. Not like a bodybuilder, but like a well-toned athlete.

The phone was ringing at his end. 'Amanda, hi.' He even said my name like the words were caramel being spooned into my ear.

I had it bad.

'Hi, Brett. Are you free to talk?'

'Absolutely, I just got back from the gym. I'm on my way to the shower, but I'm in no rush and would much rather talk to you than do anything else.' He was naked! Slutty Amanda wanted to ask him to send a selfie right now. Fortunately, the sane Amanda was in charge at the moment, so I came up with a different question instead.

'What are you doing tomorrow night?' I specifically said tomorrow night and not tomorrow evening although I wasn't sure he would pick up on the subtle nuance of the words.

'Dear lady, I will be doing whatever you tell me to do.' His voice had deepened and taken on a husky tone as he spoke. It made me think that he was thinking sex thoughts. 'It's your turn to host me for a date after all,' he added his voice back to normal and full of enthusiasm.

'Well, Brett. I was hoping you would be okay to come to my flat tomorrow. I have something special planned.' I hadn't intended to say the word *special* so breathlessly, but I did and was certain it had left no ambiguity in my intentions for the evening.

'That … err. That sounds like an event I shouldn't miss,' he said, stumbling but recovering well, the husky edge back. I could only imagine what my playful words were doing to his blood flow. I was already imagining the blood flowing somewhere very particular.

'Eight o'clock. Bring wine. I'll be waiting, lover.' The last word slid out as an intended promise.

I heard him swallow at the other end of the line. He got it. 'I'm looking forward to it already, Amanda. I will see you at eight.'

'Until then, Brett,' I breathed into the phone. My God, I was aroused already thinking about him. He bid me a very good evening and was gone. Off to get a shower, possibly a cold one.

I needed to get off the bed and think about something else. Making a shopping list/list of things to do was required, so I sat on the couch and got on with that. I needed to buy condoms for starters. He might well bring some, yet it felt better to be prepared. I needed to have food in that was easy to prepare. I needed to get a wax, but it was already too late for that, and I needed to clean the flat, wash and remake the bed linen and very possibly buy new underwear.

While I had been on the phone to Brett, I had received a call that I had of course ignored. Now that I looked though I saw it was the same number as earlier and I now had no fewer than five missed calls in the space of just over an hour. It seemed easier to call it, deal with the salesman on the other end and then block the number than it did to continue ignoring it, so I pressed dial and set my face to angry, so I would be ready to deal with the annoying person at the other end.

The voice though was that of a young woman. 'Tempest Michaels?' she asked hopefully.

'No. Amanda Harper. I'm Tempest's business partner. Can I help you?' I hoped this was a client and not a girl he met in a bar.

'I think he took my cat. I don't know what to do. He just won't leave me alone and the police won't do anything.' The words had come out in a torrent, like they had been building up, threatening to overflow and were suddenly without a barrier to hold them in place.

I tried to calm her. 'Miss, I need you to slow down. Then we need to back up a little. Can you tell me your name please?' I snagged a notepad and a pen from the coffee table and sat on the sofa.

'Sorry.' Her voice was close to a sob. 'My name is Kimberley Kousins. I'm being stalked by a Voodoo priest, and I think he may plan to kill me.'

I switched to cop mode. 'Kimberley, where are you now?'

'At home.'

'Are you by yourself and is the house secure?'

'Yes, and yes,' she answered confidently.

'Do you believe the man will attempt to force entry? Has he displayed any behaviour so far that would suggest he is violent?'

'Not so far, no. He is very scary though,' she told me.

'Okay, Kimberley. Where is home for you?'

'Maidstone, the Magdalene Estate.'

That wasn't welcome news. The Magdalene Estate in Maidstone is a lot like Mogadishu in Somalia – the shitty bit of it. During a particularly nasty turf war. Burning tyres, cars and random flying bullets were not uncommon. The people living there were not very nice generally, at least the ones you saw were not, the nicer ones stayed inside their houses hoping the world would end soon.

I had Kimberley give me her address and I promised to be there within the hour. As I hung up the phone, I considered calling Tempest to see if he had any advice, or had given any thought to the case, but I didn't. Part of me taking the job at his firm was me standing on my own feet and being able to operate on my own as an independent investigator. I would see him at the office in the morning where we could discuss this and other cases. In the meantime, I would interview the young woman and see if there was a case here or not.

The Magdalene Estate

The app on my phone claimed the outside temperature to be four degrees. It felt cooler than that and I had been shocked when I got outside to find my car not parked in its usual spot by the bins. A brief moment of panic that it had been stolen or had perhaps run away at the thought of going to the Magdalene Estate, seeped away to be replaced by shameful regret when I remembered that the car was still parked at the police station more than a mile away because I had gotten drunk for lunch.

I tussled with the idea of calling Kimberley to tell her I couldn't make it until the morning, but she'd been so grateful that I was coming I could not in good conscience now do that to her. I slung my handbag over my shoulder and started speed walking through town.

My hands were frozen by the time I got to my car, making me wish I had one with a heated steering wheel. The hot air blowers warmed up a few minutes later, so I pointed them at my knuckles, trying to balance the air flow so that some of the blissfully warm air would also hit my face and body as it defrosted my fingers.

I left the town centre on the A229, sweeping up the hill towards the village of Loose, but turned off before I reached the tranquillity of that area and entered the Estate. Magdalene was such that someone controlling the budget had decided many years ago that it was cheaper to build a small Police Headquarters there than keep dispatching units from town. Even this late at night, with the temperature outside barely above freezing there were dodgy looking youths hanging out on street corners, younger kids riding their bikes and smoking cigarettes and older kids and adults hanging out in cars, probably doing drugs. They were not all male either, lots of them were girls, but girls that looked like they might mug you or knife you. And then very possibly pee on you for good measure.

I didn't like that my car had been spotted the second I turned onto Magdalene Avenue. Laughably it was called an avenue still even though all the trees had long since been burned down or dug up. I wondered if maybe some of the trees had evolved due to necessity, grown legs and moved.

Kimberley's address placed her on the nicer side of the estate, which was to say there were fewer cars on bricks or refrigerators laying in the street outside her house. Not that she lived in a house. She had a flat in a building much like mine only nowhere near as nice. She lived at number two on the bottom floor. The curtain twitched as I got out of my car and stood looking at it, forlornly hoping it would still be there when I came out.

I hurried around the building to the entrance at the front and down the path to get inside, not willing to hang around in case I was spotted by the next gang of layabout kids. There was probably no danger to me, but dealing with them, even verbally was a task I would sooner avoid.

Inside the building's little foyer, several of the lights were out, but there was enough still working that I could read the graffiti. It was sprayed liberally on every surface like I had just walked into a breakdance club from the eighties. All that was missing was a couple of rival gangs having a dance fight and a gold-toothed DJ. Three steps led up to the first floor, a poor design given how many single mums must end up in buildings similar to this one.

The door to number two was open a crack, a slither of a face showing just above the security chain. The person inside decided that I was who they were waiting for, the door closed to the sound of the chain being rattled and then opened again to reveal a woman of about twenty-five.

Kimberly Kousins was pretty but was doing her best to hide it. Despite a pronounced overbite her face was well proportioned and covered in small pimples. True to the fashion of the area though, she wore a full face of makeup and crazy-long false eyelashes just to sit at home watching television. She stood five feet seven inches tall, making her quite average in height, her eyes were brown to match her hair which was pulled back into a ponytail, the length of which dictated that once released it would fall to just about touch her shoulders. It was also stuffed into a black diamanté ball cap. She wore huge gold hoop earrings which were filled with a bold letter K and were paired with no less than six more smaller hoops running up the edge of her left ear, but oddly none at all in her right. She had a nose piercing which was another gold hoop and around each wrist were colourful and sparkly Pandora bracelets. A brief pang of jealousy shot through me at seeing those particular items as I had coveted them through the shop window for many months now. I could buy them for myself but somehow that felt like cheating. I wanted a boy to buy the pretty trinkets for me, just like the wonderful advertisements on television.

Kimberly beckoned for me to hurry in. I felt no need to quicken my pace. There was no one else in sight, nor could I hear anyone, so I was sure I could cross the eight feet of foyer and get inside before a marauding horde descended upon us.

'Amanda Harper,' I said as I got close to her door. I was putting out my hand to shake, but she was only interested in getting me inside and shutting the door.

As I squeezed by her, I readjusted my assessment of her height and gave her an extra half inch. I also gave some consideration to her weight which I estimated to be fifty-five kilos. She wore grey flannel sportswear. The uniform of the stupid Tempest had once called it. I understood his senti-ment. Wearing a warm-up suit when not doing sports is completely fine, but I had interviewed people in my capacity as a police officer that had been wearing their favourite Sunday Best crappy grey outfit and thought they looked good.

'Please hurry,' Kimberly begged as got inside. The door all but slammed behind me. 'I don't want Mrs Hamilton to see you. She keeps telling the other neigh-bours I'm a prostitute. She will think you're my social worker.'

I didn't know whether this was an insult or not. Did I dress like a social worker?

'Will my car be safe outside?' I asked.

'God, no.'

Jolly good. So glad I checked.

'Let's make this quick then, shall we?' I asked as I took

myself to the front of the house where I could see out the window to my currently unmolested car outside.

I had arrived in her small galley kitchen. She had followed me in, looking pensive and holding her hands together as if she was about to start wringing them.

I pulled out a notebook from my handbag and clicked my pen. 'Kimberly, please tell me why you called and how it is that you think I can help.'

'Like I said on the phone, I met a man online, on a dating website and now he is stalking me. The police won't do anything, and I'm scared.'

She was bordering on hysterical, almost in tears. I wanted to calm her down so that I could better question her. 'Kimberly, why don't you put the kettle on and make two nice cups of tea?'

'I only have coffee.'

'Coffee will be fine,' I replied, wondering what kind of person didn't have the means to make a cup of tea. It was the action though, not the beverage itself that I was after. The mundanity of making a hot beverage would focus her on something else and help to re-establish a normal pulse rate. As she busied herself at the sink filling the kettle, I started asking questions.

'Kimberly let's start with a few basic pieces of information.' I found it was better to get a person talking about facts first. It established a baseline and got them into the frame of mind for answering questions. I asked her age, her profession, where she worked, where she had grown up and noted the answers on a fresh page. I kept going with the details of her life until the coffee was made. Then switched tack. 'The man's name, what is it?'

'Bartholomew King. He calls himself the Magdalene King.'

'The Magdalene King,' I repeated as I wrote.

'Ridiculous, isn't it?' she asked, a nervous laugh escaping with the question. 'I had heard of him, or at least I had heard of the Magdalene King, but I didn't know it was him until we went on a date.'

'Explain how you met please.'

'It was online. There is a dating website called *Meet Market?* Have you heard of it?' Her face coloured as she named the website. I made no comment. 'I found him on there. You can search by distance from your postcode. No point finding a guy if he is in Scotland, right?'

I indicated that I was listening and wanted her to continue.

'Well, it was me that approached him. You could say I brought this on myself. He had such a nice smile, and it said he was only a couple of miles from me. We exchanged messages for more than a week, and he was quite sweet. He talked about still living with his mum and dad and working with them as a chemist. He was very keen to meet, right from the start. He said lots of nice things, which wore down any misgivings I had.' She stopped to take a sip of her coffee and to shudder a little. Retelling her story was taking some effort.

'Go on,' I encouraged.

'Two weeks ago, we met for coffee in town, and he was still this really sweet guy. I liked his bald head, and he has a perfect smile that made me want to take my knickers off.'

I didn't write that bit down.

'I kissed him at the end of the date, and we arranged to meet each other two days later. That was where it all started going wrong.'

She paused to drink more of her coffee. I did likewise but didn't get more than the first mouthful in as it was quite awful. It was instant coffee but must have been a supermarket or budget brand. I managed to swallow the foul dishwater rather than spit it back into the mug, but I wasn't going to drink the rest of it.

'He texted me later that evening to set up the next date, but he wanted to see me the next day. I had already said that I couldn't because I had a Zumba class that evening. He wouldn't take no for an answer though and he said he had a special purpose for me and how much I was going to enjoy it. When I said I thought it best if we didn't see each other again he got quite angry.'

'Did he threaten you?'

'Not in a text message or on the dating service. The police said that because I had no evidence to show that it was anything more than a lover's quarrel, they could do nothing about it. Not even speak with him.'

'That's right, I'm afraid.'

'What do you mean?' she asked me mystified.

'The police have limited resources to appropriate to their workload and have to prioritise constantly. Inevitably, cases where there is no provable crime get very little attention. Stalker cases are very hard to prove and of course, they get lots of false reports each week.'

'But he cursed me,' she said with a sob, burying her head in her hands.

'What do you mean by that?' When she failed to answer after several seconds, I had to repeat the question. She still didn't answer and just as I was about to speak again, she reached up with one hand and pulled her ball cap from her head. Several pieces of her shoulder length brown hair fell out as she did so, and she met my gaze with a glum expression.

'He came to the house two days after I had met him in

town for coffee. He was waiting in the bushes out the front with some of his crew and ambushed me before I could get into the house. He was naked from the waist up and he had bones painted all over his skin to make him look like a skeleton. He held a small snake in one hand and a headless chicken in the other. He flicked the chicken and covered me in its blood. It was so disgusting.'

I was making notes but thinking that I really didn't want to ever meet this guy.

Kimberly had more to say. 'He kept chanting the whole time. Chanting and laughing, like it was funny to him. The rest of them were laughing too. They were blocking my path in every direction.'

'Did any of them touch you?'

'No, none of them did. I screamed at them to get out of my way, but they just laughed some more and then he clicked his fingers, and they all stopped. That's when he said I was cursed. That he'd laid a curse upon me, and I would be afflicted with ugliness for spurning him. My hair would fall out, my teeth would fall out … all that sort of thing. Then they walked away. Just walked away like it was done. I locked myself in my flat and kept expecting them to come back. But they didn't. I saw him the next day though. When I was leaving for work, he was standing on a street corner, like he was watching for me or something. He smiled and waved, but not in a friendly way.' She finished her coffee and saw that I had let mine go cold.

'Sorry, I'm not really thirsty,' I said. She didn't seem to care. She got up to put her mug in the sink. 'Kimberly, I need to fill in a few missing details. What was the date when you first made contact and when you went on the first date?'

'The first date was a Monday night, two weeks ago.'

I did some mental maths. 'The 17th?'

'If that was a Monday two weeks ago, then yes. I made first contact with him on the Saturday night a week and a couple of days before that. I'm so stupid. Why did I contact him?' I Understood the sentiment, I had asked myself the same question about a boy before.

'So, what happened after he claimed to have cursed you?'

'Nothing. At least not for a while. It was four days later when I noticed there was more hair than usual in the shower drain. I didn't think anything about it at first but the next day there was blood on my toothbrush and even more hair in the shower. I saw him every day after that. He was always somewhere different, but it was as if he knew where I was going to be. I saw him in town on my lunch break, on my drive home, outside my window at night. When it wasn't him, it was one of his awful crew of followers. By the time I gave up on hoping the police would do something and called your investigation agency my face was breaking out into spots, and my hair was coming out in clumps.' The last sentence came out between sobs. The poor girl was having a bad time of it, picked on by a gang of bullies led by a man that sounded like a real charmer. He and I would be having words in due course, but for now, I needed to wring whatever more information out of her that I could.

'Kimberly, I think I should start by ruling out the possibility that you have been cursed. Voodoo, like all supernatural legends, is nothing more than embellished stories and fantasy for the gullible. You are, however, the victim of some nasty stalking and, if you wish to engage the firm, I will do what I can to put an end to it.' It wasn't much of a case. I expected that once I had confronted the man, he would decide it was too much effort and find some other way to use his time.

'If voodoo is all fantasy, how do you explain my hair and my bleeding gums and loose teeth and my spots?' Kimberly was all snot and tears.

It was a good question. One for which I did not have an answer.

'I'm going to be ugly,' she wailed loudly. 'And he took my cat.'

I hated when the victims got all emotional. It was an unavoidable part of the job as a police officer, but I had hoped it would be a less regular event as a private investigator. Notices of bereavement, whenever I had been tasked to deliver them, had been a two-person job and I had had always positioned myself nearest the kitchen, so I could offer to make the tea and not be the one putting an arm around the bereaved. Here I was though with a sobbing, snot-dripping young woman and no chance of back up.

'Tell me about your cat. When did it go missing?' I asked by way of a distraction.

'He took her three days ago. At least that is when she went missing and she has never gone missing before. She is a two-year-old Persian with a blue-collar inset with Swarovski crystals.'

I jotted the information down. Given his trick with the chicken, I worried for the cat. 'Her name?'

'Miss Pussy,' she replied with a half giggle that escaped her lips between the sobs.

I wrote the name down without making comment. 'Are you sure she has not got locked in somewhere? Cats do that.'

'No, I can't be certain. But I would not put it past him to have taken her.' Kimberly gave herself a shake. 'Here, I have a photo for you, just in case you happen to see her.'

I slipped the photograph into the cover of my notebook,

then looked down at the pages worth of jotted lines. Plenty of detail. The question now was how to approach the case. 'Kimberly, what outcome do you want to get from this?' I asked. I had learned at some point that a lot of people reporting crimes against themselves are not seeking justice, mostly they want to offload the information and never think about it again. Some though want the perpetrator behind bars and yet others want the police, or perhaps God, or whoever is feeling most into retribution that week to deliver a broken arm or something.

Kimberly fixed me with an expression that suggested I was stupid. 'I want him to lift the curse, return my cat and leave me alone,' she stated with some frustration as if it were obvious.

Return her life to normal I wrote on my page and underlined it.

'Okay, Kimberly. I'm going to take this case, but we need to discuss fees first.' I wondered what the girl could afford. If she had any worthwhile money tucked away, she would be spending it on moving somewhere nicer. I wondered how Tempest would feel about me taking a case at a lower fee than usual. He has often said the business can't always be about profit and I had noticed in him a need to play the part of the hero when there was a woman in trouble.

I outlined to Kimberly our standard fees, watched her eyes widen and her bottom lip wobble again and offered her a discount. The discount came courtesy of her agreeing to help on the case where she could.

We settled on a rate that she could afford, and I explained what my likely next steps would be. I asked if she could go to stay with her mother or a sister or other relative, but her parents lived in Scotland and she couldn't go there and keep her job, she was an only child and had very few other relatives. I wanted her to stay in the house and thus defuse his ability to intimidate her while I gave some thought to how it was that she was losing her hair and teeth and suddenly getting spots. She wouldn't though. She had work in the morning and refused to call in sick. I didn't say it, but I was impressed by her determination to soldier on.

I could do nothing else for her tonight. I closed my note-book, put it away and promised to call her the next day with an update. I wasn't going to do anything more tonight. As I thought that, a yawn forced my mouth open. I was tired. It had been a long day already which had started at six o'clock this morning with a trip to the gym.

Kimberly showed me out, her parting comments to wish me luck and to beg me to help her once more.

I left the building, walking fast to cover the distance to my car which was around the corner of the building where the car park was situated. On the bonnet of my car were two young men.

Annoying Young Men

'All right, Darling,' said one in greeting. He was maybe eighteen, he had a can of Supertennents lager in his right hand, and he was all smiles. 'Out by yourself?'

'I reckon she looks like she needs a date, Terrance.'

'I reckon you're right, Trevor.' The two weren't drunk, I decided. They were idiots with just enough alcohol in them to make them brave. 'Is that right, sweetheart. Are you looking for a man?'

'Why? Would you like to help me find one?' I plipped the car open, my stride never slowing as I approached them. Other women might be intimidated by such behaviour. But as a police officer, I was used to dealing with mouthy, unruly, idiot teenage boys. If they didn't get off my car, I would drive away with them still on it.

'What did you say?' asked the one who had spoken first. His lecherous smile was replaced by an angry mask as he slid off the bonnet and to his feet. 'You think you're clever? How about I show you how much of a man I am? You won't walk straight for a week, babe.'

'Yeah,' his friend echoed.

Were they going to get aggressive? It was always hard to tell. They were blocking my path to the car, forcing me to stop. I could trade petty insults with them all night, but I was tired, and I wanted to get home. My right hand was fishing in my bag. Finally, I found what I had been rooting for and produced my police ID.

'Boys, if you want women to treat you like men, you need to start treating them like ladies. Go home, grow up and don't let me find you hanging around here again.'

Neither of them seemed to have a retort. It was the police ID that had quelled their tongues, not my demeanour. They were not quite done yet though.

'Gonna be watchin' for you, bitch,' Terrance sneered, his voice an insistent threat.

I slid into my car, refusing to hurry my pace or let them know that my pulse was hammering. Both men were taller, stronger and probably more willing to resort to violence than I. I had fight training, all cops do, and I had gone to additional classes, but it didn't mean that I could face down two men and feel no fear.

As I pulled away, I dared one glance back at them, just to see if they were still watching me. Terrance mimed shooting me with his right hand.

Where Do We Work Now?

I awoke with a jolt of nervousness, a dream that I could not now recall somehow scaring me awake. As my pulse returned to normal, I stared at the ceiling and remembered that I had Brett coming to the house tonight. My stomach squirmed with unnecessary worry. I had been feeling weird about Brett since the very first date, little more than two weeks ago. He was just so perfect. It's not as though I'm a virgin, for goodness sake. Why was I making such a big deal out of spending the night with him?

I knew the answer of course. It was because I was getting older now and thoughts of husbands and babies, that a few years ago were abhorrent, were now palatable. Brett had everything. Money, intelligence, money, wit, money, a great body, a handsome face, and money. Not that I ever thought of myself as material or mercenary. I wasn't after him because he was rich. The truth is that he pursued me, but now that the money was on the table, I had to consider it, and it was nice to consider.

I would like to say that I love my job and would

33

continue doing it even if I was rich, but I have only just started doing my new job as an investigator and would most likely quit and spend my time divided between the spa and the gym and the salon if I had the option to do so. I'm a girly girl. I like unicorns and pink things, and I like Brett Barker, so tonight I was going to show him the time of his life.

With that insistent instruction echoing in my head, I swung my legs out of bed and pointed them at the bathroom. Before I could think about entertaining Brett, I had a day ahead of me. There was a case to solve, probably other cases waiting, and this was day one of my new life where I was no longer a police officer but a private investigator instead.

The Blue Moon office burned down last week, so it seemed we would be using Tempest's house as a temporary office for a while. James had said that Tempest was away but not where he'd gone. It was a little early to call Tempest now, so I would make the call later when I had eaten breakfast and after my trip to the gym.

Five minutes later, I was going out the door in my gym gear with an oversized hoody to keep me warm against the October air.

I came back through the door of my apartment just over an hour later with the hoody stuck to my sweaty skin. I had forced myself to lift weights again. Kettlebell squats are the only way to keep a toned bum a fitness instructor had once assured me. Then showed me her fifty-year-old perfectly rounded, Lycra-clad bottom. She was right, unfortunately, and I had to do deadlifts to keep my hams and quads in order and shoulder presses to keep my arms and shoulders toned and bench press to keep the muscular wall beneath my boobs tight, which she assured me would mean they pointed the right direction for longer. I didn't hate going to the gym, I just struggled to find the motivation most days.

The biggest problem fuelling my reluctance is getting out of my sweaty sports bra after the workout. It sticks to my skin, creating resistance when my arms are already sore and don't wish to be held over my head. I swear a strait-jacket would be easier to take off. Tugging and swearing, the bathroom already filling with steam from my shower, I finally pulled it over my head and threw it in the laundry basket.

I took my time in the shower, making sure I tended to areas that Brett hadn't yet seen. All too soon, it was time to get on with the day. I ate a bowl of cereal while I was getting dressed and went out the door.

In the car park, I remembered that I didn't know where I was going and fished in my bag for my phone. I needed to call Tempest and find out where we were working from now. Just as I touched it, the phone sprang to life with an incoming call – from Tempest.

'Hi, Tempest. I was just about to call you. Where are we working from now?'

'Good morning, Amanda,' he replied.

'Good morning, Tempest. I was heading to work but realised that I don't know where we will do that now. What can I do for you?'

'I needed to let you know that I'm going to be away for a few days. I decided I needed some time off.' He fell silent while I considered his information.

'What about the business?' I asked.

'I have no live cases, Jane can handle calls and emails, and I will be back at the end of the week. If you wish to tackle anything that comes up, please feel free to do so. Jane can handle the paperwork and billing.'

'Really? Just like that? Where will Jane be working? The office got burned down.'

'I bought new IT gear and office supplies and set her up in my house. The customers will not be able to tell the difference until they wish to arrange a meeting. I asked Jane to put everyone off until the end of the week.'

'Okay. I guess that all makes sense. Tempest?'

'Yes?'

'Tempest, look. I wanted to talk about what happened with the Klowns ...' Tempest felt that I had betrayed him, or at least that was how he'd expressed it. I had been under strict instruction to not let him know that CI Quinn had assigned two plainclothes policemen to follow him. I hadn't realised he was being used as bait. I had been told they were for his protection, but in hindsight, I should have known that CI Quinn was lying to me. Now I wanted to clear the air. I liked Tempest and we were going to work together now.

He cut me off before I could express any of that though. 'Amanda, I really don't want to talk about it. Not now at least. Let's pick it up when I get back, okay?'

'Okay, Tempest. Have a good week,' I replied, stifling a yawn. We said goodbye and disconnected. Maybe Tempest and I would talk about it later. Maybe it would just be left alone. He seemed to have moved on from it.

So, I was heading to Tempest's house where I would find Jane but no Tempest. In my head, I was calling this day one of my job at the Blue Moon Investigation Agency. Even though I had already solved one case and worked on a couple of others, it had been part-time in between my shifts for the police. Now though, I was full time working with

Tempest; he insisted I was working with him, not for him. It felt like an insignificant use of words, but it was important to him somehow.

I fired up my Mini Cooper and pointed it towards his place in Finchampstead. The sky was grey today, overcast and threatening rain much the same as it had been for the last few days. The weatherman had promised thunderstorms in the area, which might make the Halloween celebrations stunted. Parents wouldn't take their children out to watch the parade in town if it was raining, nor would they want to be out trick or treating door to door.

The drive to Tempest's place took less than ten minutes despite the early morning rush hour traffic. This was mostly because I could take less-travelled country roads to get there, but it was also only a few miles from my apartment in the town centre.

His car was quite visibly absent from his drive. In its place was Jane's Ford Fiesta. The engine block was audibly cooling, quiet pinging noises coming from under the bonnet as I walked by it to tell me Jane had only recently turned the engine off.

I almost knocked on the front door but lowered my hand as I saw the pointlessness of the action. Instead, I turned the handle and let myself in. I could hear the kettle beginning to bubble its excitement in his kitchen, then Jane came into view. She heard the door open no doubt.

'Tea or coffee?' she called through from the kitchen.

'I replied with, 'Tea, please,' as I joined her, dumping my handbag on the counter as I went. 'It feels weird here without the dogs.'

Jane shrugged. 'I only came here for the first time yesterday and Tempest was about to leave then. What do you make of it? Tempest, taking a week off suddenly, I mean?' Jane asked as she was pouring the hot water.

I opened my mouth to reply, but I wasn't sure what I wanted to say. I was disappointed. He hired me, this was my first full week at the firm, the office burned down three days ago, and I was now supposed to work out of his house.

'I expect he felt that he needed a few days off. The Klown case was a tough one.' I left it at that.

Jane handed me a hot mug of tea and left the room, heading for the dining room Tempest used as a home office. 'We have a few cases to look at,' she said as I followed her.

'Is one of them something to do with voodoo?'

'How do you know that?' she asked, spinning her head around to look at me.

'Kimberly Kousins called me last night. She had been trying to get hold of Tempest, but I guess she couldn't and found my number instead. I went to see her.'

'Wow. What did you think?'

'About the case? I think Kimberly is scared and that there is a man stalking her.'

'She said she'd been cursed with ugliness and her hair and teeth were falling out.'

'Yes, that is what she told me as well. I can confirm that she was having some issues with her hair, and she said her gums were bleeding. Her skin was suffering also - lots of pimples. There is definitely something to investigate there. I already agreed to take the case.'

'Jolly good,' Jane replied, settling herself in front of the shiny new computer Tempest had bought. The box for it, along with boxes for the new printer/copier and other equipment were stacked in the corner of the room, waiting to be disposed of. 'I'm poised to do whatever research you feel necessary. There are other cases though.'

'Show me please'

For the next twenty minutes, Jane and I went through the emails, calls, and messages that had come through over the weekend. Most of them were rubbish, but as always there were one or two that held merit. One of which was from the manager of Tonbridge Wells Ghost tours. The lady's name was Lily Hallett, and she claimed they now had a real ghost. The ghost tour went around some of the older parts of Tonbridge Wells town centre, where the guide told stories and they had a few surprises where, with good timing, they were able to draw screams from their audience by having figures jump out on them or make noises in the dark. Recently they had been finding the audience screaming when they were not expected to. Several customers had reported being touched by something unseen in the dark

It was interesting enough that I copied the woman's number into my phone and called her. It rang for a few seconds before a voice came on the phone with a distinct Tonbridge Wells accent. She could not have been more posh if she tried.

'Good morning. Lily Hallett speaking.'

'Mrs Hallett. This is Amanda Harper calling from the Blue Moon Investigation Agency. I believe you have a ghost on your ghost tour and would like us to investigate.'

'Thank you for calling, Miss Harper. Is Tempest available to take my case?' Tempest has explained the sense in tackling several cases simultaneously. Most cases were only simple to solve after you had solved them. Finding the perfectly rational explanation often took hours of research and investigation though, so it was best to have overlapping cases that would allow some time for thought in between them and the time for information to be gathered. Tempest always had more than one case on the go.

'We are,' I replied, meaning the business. 'I need to meet with you so that I might begin the process of gathering information. When would be convenient? Are you able to meet with me today?'

'I have an opening this morning if you are able to come to my office in Royal Tonbridge Wells.' She made a point of saying *Royal*, just in case I wasn't aware of the town's full title. I'd never heard anyone bother to say it before, even though it's on all the road signs.

I checked my watch. It was twenty minutes after nine. I wanted to start looking into the voodoo case for Kimberly and I wanted to drop by the station to see Patience and have her check some information on Bartholomew, but I also wanted to bill some hours for the ghost tour case as it seemed likely that Mrs Hallett could afford it. I outlined our fees, which she would most likely have already read from our website and promised to meet her at her office at eleven o'clock. Mrs Hallett sounded very content that I was able to react quickly.

With the call complete, I turned my attention back to Jane and picked up my tea to drink as it was now getting cool. 'We need to look into Bartholomew King and Meet Market,' I said as I emptied the mug and placed it on the dining table out of the way.

'Bartholomew King'. Jane recited as she typed. 'Who is he?'

'He is the person Kimberly claims has cursed her. The police registered a complaint from her when her cat went missing. She accused him of taking it, but she has no evidence. I will head to the station when I leave here and see if he has a record. She makes him sound like a dirtbag and he is from the Magdalene Estate so has probably been in trouble many times. I intend to find out a bit more about him and then visit him in uniform. I still have it, so I might as well make good use of it. I expect that a stern warning will be sufficient to get him to leave Kimberly alone.'

Jane nodded in agreement, then squinted at the screen. 'You have his address wrong. It says here he lives in Bearsted. Nice postcode.'

I leaned in to look as Jane switched to Google Earth and pulled up images of the street. We couldn't tell which of the houses he lived in, but the postcode could show us the houses in that street, and they were all big, expensive places.

'Wow,' I said almost as an involuntary reaction. I knew Bearsted. There were several very lovely restaurants there and a lot of expensive properties that surrounded a large village green where one could watch a Sunday cricket match. It was the kind of village that attracted rich businessmen from London as they could commute to work each day on a direct line into the city centre but come home every night to a family living in the countryside. It wasn't unusual for there to be Lamborghinis or Ferraris parked outside people's houses. It was absolutely not in keeping with the image I had for the young man that Kimberly claimed had cursed her. 'Are you sure you have the right person?' I asked.

'I could have it wrong. We only have limited data, but he is the only Bartholomew King living in the Southeast of England. There are only three people with that name in the United Kingdom, so I figure I must have the right guy.'

'Can you email me his address, please? I will see what I can find out at the station and probably go there later today.' Jane clicked a few keys, and my phone pinged at the arrival of the email. 'Can you look at Meet Market? I want to see what kind of website it is, see if we can find his profile.'

Jane started clicking the mouse again. 'You ever try online dating?' she asked.

'No. thought about it once or twice. Wondered if I could filter out some of the idiots before I wasted an evening talking to them in a dreary bar somewhere. I never got around to it though. You?'

'Once or twice. They are good for hook-ups, but I doubt many people find their true love using a website.' Talking to Jane, I often forgot that beneath the perfume, makeup and dress is a man. He sounds like a man, of course. He doesn't try to hide his deep voice, but he looks and acts like a girl most of the time. Like a man though, he was probably able to have emotionless sex with a perfect stranger and think nothing of it, so hook-ups might be appealing to him. They were certainly not to me.

'I'm going to leave you with that to research and head off to see what I can find out about Bartholomew King.' Given the disparity in the addresses, I wondered if maybe the chap Kimberly was being stalked by had used a fake name. I would find out soon enough.

'Sure thing,' Jane replied, without looking up. She seemed quite content to do research sitting in the home office, so I collected my bag, pulled out my car keys and headed off to visit Patience.

Maidstone Police Station

The station was on the far side of the town centre from where I was at Tempest's house and a little more than a mile from my house, which I had to pass on my way there. I still had the chip in my car to access the car park behind the station, and I was officially still employed, so I parked my car as near to the door as I could get and went inside.

No one paid me any attention as I sat at an available desk and booted up the computer on it.

'Hey, girl,' came a familiar voice from behind me. I didn't have to turn around to see who it was, I already knew that it was Patience, but I could hear her coming my way, being abusive to men as she made her way across the room. 'Want a doughnut?' she asked as she arrived by my right elbow.

Patience had a coffee cup in her right hand and two doughnuts in her left. One of them had several bite marks in it. There was a trace of icing sugar on her top lip and a few sprinkles on her uniform. The uniform was looking a little snug.

'That was a rhetorical question, wasn't it?'

'Yup.' Patience wasn't known for sharing her confections. 'What are you doing here anyway? I thought you quit this job.' Patience put her coffee down, shoved the remainder of the half-eaten doughnut in her mouth and pulled up a chair.

'I need to look someone up on the database. My latest case involves a young lady that lives on the Magdalene Estate. She has a stalker of sorts, and I want to check his record.' A thought occurred to me. 'You have heard of the Magdalene King, right?'

'Of course. Everyone has. Might be a legend, might be real. No one really knows.'

'The client believes her stalker is the Magdalene King.'

'Isn't that legend a few decades old now?'

'Maybe it was a legend and now it's not. Anyway, I need to find this chap and see what kind of record he has.' I clicked the mouse a couple of times, navigated to a new screen, and typed in his name. The page spooled for about a second before a young, handsome, black man's face filled the left half of the screen. He looked like a college athlete; all he needed was his varsity top. He was smooth shaven, but not just his face, his head was completely bald as well. It was the same man Kimberly had shown me a photograph of last night, but in her photo, he was smiling. On the right half of the screen were details regarding his past.

'Looks like your boy likes to do a bit of stalking,' observed Patience. 'Arrested in January last year but released without charge.' She was reading from the screen. I printed the page and put it in my bag. 'Hold on,' Patience started. 'This doesn't sound very supernatural. Why are you looking into it?'

'He thinks he is a voodoo priest. He cursed her with

ugliness and now her hair is falling out and she has pimples,'
I replied, starting to get up. Then I noticed Patience's face -
it had stopped moving. There was a piece of half-chewed
doughnut in there that was visible because her jaw was
hanging open. 'Are you okay?' I asked her.

Slowly, she cleared her mouth and swallowed. 'V-v-v-
voodoo,' she stammered. 'You can't go messing with
voodoo, Amanda.' She never called me Amanda. 'It's a
shame about your client, but you have to leave this one
alone.' She was dead serious.

'Patience, there is no such thing as voodoo. All I need to
do is investigate the case, work out what is happening with
her hair and face, and stop Mr King from bothering her.
I'm going to his house right now to have a little chat with
him. I'm sure that's all it will take.'

Her eyes were bugging right out of her head. She darted
forward, grabbed my handbag, and shoved her arm inside
it. Thrown off-balance, I almost fell over while she was
rooting around.

'A-ha!' she announced, coming away with my keys in
her hand. 'Patience is gonna save you from your own
stupidity this time. You ain't messing with no voodoo on my
watch, girl.'

'Give me my keys,' I demanded, cutting my eyes at her.

'Na-uh. You need to rethink your plan. Voodoo is real,
girl, and you can't go messing with those that know the art.'

'Patience what are you talking about?'

As she opened her mouth to answer my question I
leaped forward, grabbing for my keys. She danced away and
got a desk between us.

Other people in the room had turned away from what
they had been doing so they could watch us.

'Patience, I don't have time for this. Give me my keys.' I

made another grab for them, but each time I tried to close the distance she just hopped out of the way. I dumped my bag and climbed on the desk.

Patience saw me go vertical and ran for the door. I had to run across the room using the desks as steppingstones. My foot caught someone's coffee spill though, and I slid, arms cartwheeling, and down I went. As I fell, I caught sight of Patience reaching the door. She was looking back at me and failed to notice CI Quinn coming through it. She barrelled into him and knocked him flying just as I was crashing to the carpet.

The entertaining spectator sport ended abruptly as a roar from CI Quinn silenced the laughter that had filled the room a second ago. 'Woods, get off me!'

'Yes, Chief,' I heard her meek reply.

'Get up, Harper! I saw you too. The rest of you get back to work.' CI Quinn's voice took less than a second to return to its usual unflappably calm tone. I levered myself off the floor.

'What are you doing here, Harper? Back already? New job not what you thought? Or have you failed at that and been fired already?' CI Quinn never overtly picked on me. He was always cold towards me though, and, it seemed, always looked for something hurtful to say.

'My keys, Patience,' I asked again, holding out my hand.

'Don't mess with no voo ...' She was silenced by CI Quinn holding his hand in front of her face. It was something he did all too often and mostly with the women officers. Patience shot him a glance but handed over my keys with some reluctance while mouthing that I should go home and abandon the case.

'Should I expect to see you in here again, Miss Harper?'

The Chief was making a point that I was no longer part of the team.

'No, Ian,' I answered using his first name. He stiffened visibly as he considered how to reply.

'Make sure that I don't.' He stared at me. He wasn't going to be the one that turned and walked away. So, I had to.

It was easy to dislike him.

Rain began to fall outside; a light drizzle that was dampening the street. It matched my mood though I forced myself to brighten. I no longer had to put up with CI Quinn and his attitude. I slid behind the wheel of my car and joined the traffic heading out of town.

The Home of a Voodoo Priest

The drive to the small village of Bearsted, just outside Maidstone, took twelve minutes. Traffic was light, as I had expected it would be, allowing me to sweep through Penenden Heath without pausing. At rush hour, the journey would take more than an hour. The address for the house was right on the village green. On a summer day, the green would have children playing on it, pre-school age toddlers laughing and running and perhaps people out walking their dogs. In the drizzle that was falling now, the green was utterly deserted. I found the house just a couple of properties along from the restaurant that dominated one corner of the green.

I had to use the word property even when mentally referring to the houses around the village as they were all large, bespoke, imposing places. Then I remembered Brett's house. These places would be the groundsman's cottage at his stately home. Nevertheless, a person needed to part with several million to buy one, so all the local residents were doing okay for themselves.

I was arriving unannounced and had no way of knowing if anyone would be in to receive me. I was speculating that there would be as it had the potential to bring a swift end to the case – or at least a partial end. If I could stop Bartholomew from stalking Kimberly, I was halfway home. I would then need to work out what was going on with her hair and face and teeth, however, I suspected it would prove to be psychosomatic.

I parked in the street, right in front of their property and dashed through the pedestrian gate to get to the front door. Even the door was double height and double width and surely designed to make people feel small. My question regarding whether I would get lucky and find someone in was soon answered. A tall, elegant black lady answered the door. She wore a business suit with trousers in a striking dark blue and a gorgeous pair of tan leather Christian Louboutin shoes, their red soles teasing me with their perfection. Her blouse top looked to be silk and the whole ensemble was quietly telling the observer that the lady had money and knew where to spend it.

'Good morning. Mrs King, is it? My name is Amanda Harper, I hoped I could have a few minutes of your time to talk to you about your son, Bartholomew.'

She raised an eyebrow at my mention of her son. 'Are you the police?' she asked.

I was on dodgy ground suddenly. If I said that I wasn't, I would be lying. 'I'm a serving police officer, but I'm not here in any official capacity.' I decided to stick with the truth. 'I work for a private investigation agency and my presence here today is to represent the concerns of a client.'

She seemed to consider that for a moment, then opened the door wider. 'You had better come in, Miss Harper.'

I thanked her and followed her through the house. The

house was immaculate, what mine would be if I could afford to hire a cleaner. There was no dust on any surfaces and every piece of furniture, every soft furnishing looked expensive. I wondered what they did for a living.

I didn't have to wonder for long though as Mrs King started talking as she walked me through the house. 'You're lucky to catch us here. Normally my husband and I would be meeting with clients or suppliers or in a meeting at one of our facilities. We are both Chemists. We met at University in Haiti, you're probably thinking that I don't sound like I come from Haiti, and you would be right. My husband does though. I was out there on an exchange opportunity between the two universities, and he followed me back here. We set up a business together and have been quite successful.'

Quite successful was an understatement.

'Have you lived here long?' I asked, making conversation. We were still walking through her house. I had no idea where we were going, but it was taking a while to get there.

'Do you mean, in this house? Or in Bearsted? I grew up not far from here, we bought the house twenty years ago. It was already a good size, but we have added to it since we moved in. We needed an office wing for my husband and me and for little Barty of course. Not that he is little anymore. Tell me, please. What is it that he is being accused of? I can't believe he will be guilty, no matter what it is.'

The lady had failed to give me her name, and I had failed to look it up. I made a mental note to do better research in the future. She was pleasant and engaging though, someone that engendered trust. Was that why she had been so successful in her career?

As I opened my mouth to begin answering her question, we turned right, left the corridor we had been in to arrive in an office. It was a large and well-appointed room with several desks set out with computers on them. At our arrival, a man turned from his workstation, smiled and came across the room. 'Angelica, I was wondering where you had got to. Who is your friend?' he asked. His voice had a playful, sing-song tone to it that made me want to believe he would be an excellent singer.

'George this is Amanda Harper, she is a private investigator. Her client has made accusations about Barty.' At least now I knew both of their names.

'Really?' he replied, turning his gaze from his wife to me. 'I think we had better sit down and hear all about it.'

I had been mildly concerned that they wouldn't take my presence, or the suggestion their son was less than perfect, very well. Thankfully, they were treating me as a person that deserved respect. They led me to an arrangement of chairs and indicated for me to sit as they each took a seat.

It was Angelica that started speaking first, 'So, Miss Harper…'

'Angelica, let's be friends here, call her Amanda,' George interrupted, smiling at his wife.

She smiled back at him and started again, 'Amanda, please tell us what it is that has caused you to seek us out.'

'Thank you. I received a call last night from a young lady by the name of Kimberly Kousins.' I watched to see if their faces reacted to the name. If they recognised it at all they hid it well. I told them about her relationship with their son and her belief that he'd cursed her. While I was speaking, they looked at me, never at each other and pulled various expressions. It was disbelief when I told them about the online dating and humour when I used the word voodoo. They stayed silent though until I was finished.

'So, I'm here to speak with your son in the hope that this can be resolved amicably.'

Now that I was done, they both moved in their chairs to face one another. 'I have to say, wife, that this all sounds very unlikely.'

'I agree, George. I doubt that Bartholomew has had anything to do with this lady at all.'

'And the voodoo thing has to be nonsense, surely.'

I watched their conversation, letting them convince themselves that their child couldn't be guilty. It was possible they were right, of course, I had no evidence either way, only the word of Kimberly that he was involved at all. But he'd been accused before. I could feel I was going to have to remind them of that. They were still discussing him though, so I kept quiet rather than interrupt.

'He's so loyal to Patrice, and he's never been in trouble.'

'Well, there was the one time that the police saw fit to investigate him.' It was George who brought it up. 'He didn't do it, but he was accused of stalking then as well.'

'Yes, but he didn't do it,' Angelica stated with a hint of venom. 'All the charges were dropped two days later.' She turned to me. 'I'm sorry, Amanda. We are ignoring you. It wasn't our intention to be rude. Can I show you something?' she asked getting up.

I moved to follow her, but she waved for me to stay where I was. 'I need just a second,' she said. She left the room but returned less than five seconds later holding a framed photograph. I could see what it was before she reached the sitting area. It was a graduation photograph of Bartholomew.

'Our son has a borderline genius I.Q. He achieved a double first at Kings College Oxford in Chemistry and Advanced Physical Chemistry. He is engaged to a woman he has been dating since he was a teenager, and I can assure you that he has had nothing to do with your client.' George remained quiet. 'I believe this can all be cleared up quite easily so the simplest thing for me to do is tell you where he is and let you resolve this with him. I don't feel the need for George and me to be involved. The Kimberly girl is clearly deluded or confused. Do you agree George?' she asked, turning to her husband.

'Yes, Dear. Bartholomew is a man, not a boy. He can take care of his own business without needing us to protect him.'

'Thank you for your cooperation and understanding.' Angelica and George were the nicest people I had ever met. They were reacting in direct contrast to what I had expected. My role in the police had seen me deliver miscreant children of all ages back to their parents and I had never been met by such calmness.

'I just need a moment to call him, dear,' Angelica excused herself as she got up once more. She took a few paces away, a phone to her ear. I couldn't hear her conversation, but it felt like my time at their house was coming to an end, so I began gathering my items into my bag in readiness to leave. Angelica and George acted as if they were completely certain that Bartholomew had to be innocent. They were so convincing in fact that I was beginning to doubt his guilt myself. I would speak with him, but unless I found some convincing evidence, I was going to have to return to Kimberly and question her again. Had she made it all up? It was Halloween after all – maybe this was an elaborate trick.

I remained seated throughout the conversation, but when I heard Angelica disconnect, I stood up, ready to leave.

'Bartholomew is expecting you. He is, of course, innocent and will be happy to go on record or make a statement, or whatever it is that will clear his name and end your investigation. He is at a friend's house in Maidstone. You can find him there directly. Is that convenient?'

'You mean, can I go there now?'

'Yes, dear.'

'All I need is an address, please.'

Angelica strode across the room to a desk, her elegant heels clicking lightly on the tiled floor. The door to the room, the one we had come in through, was in the same direction so I began walking after her, watching as she selected a slip of paper from a pad and jotted down an address for me.

While I waited for her to finish, I spotted another door in the corner of the room to my left. It was partially hidden behind a whiteboard on which a complex chemical compound was written over almost the entire board. I couldn't tell what it was for but recognised what it was from classes at Uni and back in school. The door led to a set of stairs that disappeared downwards into the darkness beyond. Angelica had said this was an extension to the original house for them to add offices. I wondered what was in the basement level they had added. Probably a wine cellar.

Angelica stood up and turned to me, brandishing the slip of paper which she had folded neatly. 'Good luck with your endeavours, Miss Harper,' she said as she handed it over. 'I will show you out.'

I slipped the paper into my pocket after quickly checking the address for myself as we left the room. It was on the Magdalene Estate.

'Goodbye, my dear,' George called after me.

'Goodbye, Mr King,' I replied, but I was already out of

the room and being led through the vast warren of corridors and rooms that would take me back to the front door.

As sunlight flooded through the open front door, I saw that it had stopped raining. I turned to thank Angelica for her assistance once more but stopped as I heard a vehicle next to me. Its diesel engine was rumbling along the side of the house to my left. Then it appeared, a small van being driven by a man sporting long dreadlocks. His dark skin was pockmarked by acne that had cleared up but had left his face damaged. The van had no markings on it to indicate it was part of a national chain.

'Deliveries,' Angelica said, following my gaze. 'George and I need chemicals here to conduct our research.'

I nodded, fixing her with a smile. It was none of my business and she'd been more helpful than I could have hoped for. I thanked her once again and went back out the front gate to my car. In the quiet and very lovely village of Bearsted, my car was exactly as I had left it. I wondered if it would get the same treatment back on the Magdalene Estate where I was heading yet again.

Not What I Expected

I was getting hungry when I arrived at the address I had for Bartholomew. According to Angelica, it was the house of a good friend of Bartholomew's. A person he'd gone to school with many years ago. I was finding it hard to imagine how he could have ever moved in the same circles as the person living in the house in front of me, but I had no reason to disbelieve what I had been told.

On the way, I had called Lily Hallett and explained that I was delayed dealing with another case and asked if we could rearrange our meeting. I was expecting her to be snippy with me for breaking our arrangement, however, she seemed satisfied that I had taken the time to call her and advised that I would be tied up. She said that Tempest and I would be able to find her at the ghost tours office in *Royal* Tonbridge Wells all afternoon. It was impossible to predict how my current case would pan out, but I intended to meet with her today, so that was what I told her. She seemed quite keen that Tempest be involved but I saw no reason to explain that he was out of town.

I parked my car around the corner from Mason's house. Right in front of the house was a shiny, new-looking Nissan GTR. The number plate read K1NGS. It had to be Bartholomew's. I could have parked next to it but there were no other cars about, and the house bordered a park, so my car would be very visible. Around the corner, it was tucked against a rotting fence and behind a van where I hoped it would remain out of sight.

The doorbell was broken so I knocked on the door. To my left and right were discarded free papers that might be months old. They were sun-bleached and tatty. Weeds, crisp packets and other small pieces of litter were caught in the few plants desperately clinging to life in the front garden. The whole house had an abandoned look to it, but a shadow moved through the light behind the frosted glass of the front door, and I could hear music coming from within the house.

The name of the friend, the owner of the house I was knocking on, was Mason Armitage. I knew nothing about him but assumed his approximate age to be that of Bartholomew's. I also assumed he would be Haitian, or Afro Caribbean so imagine my surprise when a skinny white kid answered the door.

It was the same skinny white kid with greasy dreadlocks I had chased down for stealing purses yesterday. He was out already and was now stood leering at me from the doorway. I reached into my handbag for a business card. I would stay professional.

'Mason Armitage?' I enquired.

'Nah, love. He's inside. Come in, you're expected.'

The house smelled of marijuana. That was the first thing I noticed. The house was a typical semi-detached place. There would be a lounge and dining room coming off the corridor to my left and a kitchen dead ahead. Up the stairs on the right would be three small bedrooms and a joint bathroom and toilet. I had been in dozens, if not hundreds of these houses. Many of which were on this estate.

I followed the skinny white kid into the lounge through the first door on our left. The room was mostly in darkness; the curtains were drawn to shut out the daylight. Someone had turned the music off and now the room was silent. Two dozen faces were staring at me. I spotted Bartholomew nestled on a long sofa against the far wall from the doorway in which I was now stood. He was naked from the waist up and smoking a large joint. Either side of him were two women, their dark skin almost merging with the black leather of the sofa in the dim light. They were both stripped down to their underwear. Around the room, most of the other occupants were only partially dressed, though thankfully no one had their junk hanging out, and many of them were smoking. The room was filled with the heavy, cloying, sweet stench of marijuana.

The skinny white kid had gone into the room ahead of me. He took up a position at Bartholomew's feet. Like a dog might. Bartholomew reached forward to pat him on the head.

Everyone was still staring at me, no one was speaking. It was quite unnerving, but I wasn't going to let my rising fear show. 'Bartholomew King?' I said as I tried to make my way across the room to shake his hand. I had to go slow; there were legs and feet and hands on the carpet where the occupants had spilled from the furniture to the carpet.

I didn't get to cross the room though before he started speaking. 'You dare to disturb my parents?' his voice was calm, the accent educated, but the tone carried malice. 'Insolent white bitch.' I sooo loved being called names.

'Bartholomew, I think you and I need to have a little chat.' I wanted to extricate him from the crowd of people around him, but I was beginning to worry that wouldn't happen. Clearly, he wasn't as innocent and well-behaved as his parents liked to think. 'Shall we go through to the kitchen?' It felt like a futile request when I said it. I really wanted to leave, but I was here now and had a good chance to deal with my client's case if I could just get him alone and talk some sense into him.

'Woman,' he started, still utterly relaxed and laying back on the sofa. 'Woman you have done me wrong, but I will forgive you, for you are beautiful.' He leaned forward, locking eyes with me and smiling. 'Come upstairs with me now and you can be Bartholomew's woman.'

No thanks.

A hand brushed my leg. I jolted in reaction and spun my head around to see who it was in the dark. When I looked back at Bartholomew a heartbeat later, he was off the sofa and only a few feet away from me. He was reaching out with his hand to take mine.

'Woman let us join ourselves now. To say no would be truly dread.'

I thought about taking his hand and leading him from the room. It seemed like a safe way to get him away from his friends, who were creeping me out with the continued silence. When I didn't respond immediately, he grabbed my left arm, pinning it with a strong grip.

I reached my right hand across, dug my thumbnail into the soft flesh between his thumb and forefinger to break the grip then turned his wrist against itself. As I forced him to the floor at my feet, everything in the room changed.

At once, everyone was on their feet. Adrenalin caused my heart rate to rocket, but no one moved towards me. 'Can I let go of you, Bartholomew? Will you behave?' I asked. I was terrified, surrounded by a crowd of people and hoping that I could keep the fear from my voice. Maybe if I sounded like I was the one in charge they wouldn't do anything foolish. Then I remembered my police ID.

Using my free hand, I reached into my bag to find it. 'I must warn you that I'm a police officer ...'

'That will not save you, woman,' Bartholomew said from his position at my feet. He began chanting. A low eerie noise using words I couldn't understand. Around me, the crowd in the room began to sway. A woman let out a whoop. Looking around, my panic threatening to over-whelm me, I could see that their eyes had rolled back into their heads. Every one of them was showing me white eyes. It was freaking freaky, and I was scared enough to call it a day.

I dropped Bartholomew's arm, letting him regain his feet as I backed towards the door. No one tried to stop me, so I turned and ran. 'I curse you,' Bartholomew called after me. As I ran, I felt a tug on my scalp like something or someone had snagged my hair.

I reached the front door, turned the handle and damned near fell out of the house into the thankful daylight outside.

'I curse you, woman. I curse you with a plague of snakes and spiders. You will perish this very week.' His voice carried down the street as I ran to my car. 'Please convey to Kimberly that she has made her predicament worse.'

I risked a glance over my shoulder to make sure I wasn't being followed and almost sobbed with relief when I saw no one behind me. I reached the end of the row of houses and turned the corner to get back to my car. I was fumbling in my bag for my keys but couldn't locate them with my panicked hand. With my other hand, I held the bag open to peer inside as I ran.

Consequently, I wasn't looking where I was going and failed to see what was waiting for me.

'Going somewhere, bitch?'

It was Terrance and Trevor. They were both sitting on the bonnet of my car again. This time though they had brought about twenty of their friends with them.

Not the Best Day Ever

My heart rate was still calming down after escaping Mason's house and now I had these morons to deal with. I wasn't in the mood. I whipped out my police ID. I was going to get them off my car and drive away.

Terrance had other ideas though. 'Don't think that ID will save you this time blondie. You disrespected the Magdalene Massif. No one does that.'

'Yeah,' said Trevor.

'You need to pay a toll.'

'Yeah,' said Trevor.

I was wishing I had my baton with me, or perhaps a gun. The twenty or so young men that were with Trevor and Terrance had begun to fan out to surround me. Once again, I was getting thoroughly uncomfortable. This wasn't a safe situation. I turned to retreat along the road. I would run for it if I had to, but my path was blocked. There were even more of them behind me.

'Now then,' started Terrance, his voice full of confidence and good humour. 'What sort of toll do you think we should make the lady pay?' he asked the crowd.

I turned back to face him. 'You had better enjoy this, Terrance. In a short while you're going to be in a cell. Do you really want to assault a police officer?'

'Oh, blondie. I'm not going to assault you. Far from it. I'm going to give you the chance to perform a simple task.' He patted his groin, making it abundantly obvious what the simple task was. 'Now, I know there is a lot of it,' he said as he unzipped his fly. 'But we already know that you have a big mouth ...'

I slumped my shoulders in resignation. All his entourage were jeering and making filthy noises of encouragement. I hiked my bag onto my shoulder and moved towards him. Encouraged, Terrance took out what he had for me.

I grabbed hold of it with both hands (not that it was big enough to need both hands. I just wrapped my right hand around the left) and tried to lift him off the ground.

'You dirty little stain!' I screamed in his face. As his friends leapt to get me off him, I let go and kneed him hard in his nuts.

Then hands were grabbing me and there were too many of them to fight. I struggled and punched and kicked at anything I could get to, but no more than a couple of seconds later I was hauled off the pavement and into the air, my limbs no longer mine to control.

Panic was rising. I had made so much noise that people had to have heard. I needed someone to call the police and get them here before I was bundled into a car or a house and lost from sight. Then, I was falling. The young men had let go of me and were swearing and yelling about something new.

Had the police arrived already?

'Take that, tiny person!'

Hold on. I know that voice. I spun myself around on the pavement where I had painfully come to land. There, in front of me, was Big Ben. He was standing on the inert forms of three or four different young men, had another one hanging limply from his left hand which was wrapped around the smaller man's throat and was looking for someone else to hit.

'Come on, boys. Is that all you've got? There is only one of me,' he goaded. 'Come on, have another go.'

'Having fun, Benjamin?' I asked.

He turned to look at me, dropping the possibly dead man from his grip. 'Hello, Amanda.' He offered me his hand to help me up. I was soggy from rolling in a puddle and had bits of leaf litter in my hair. 'Shall we go?'

'I should call the police and have these *gentlemen* rounded up.'

'Well… I might have accidentally killed one or two of them. I didn't think I had hit them that hard, but they haven't moved for a while, so if it's alright with you, I think I would rather just leave.'

The crowd of boys had scattered. No one able to stand was still in sight so it was going to be problematic finding them. Big Ben might have a point about the damage sustained. there were at least seven men on the ground that were not moving. Then I spotted Terrance, trying to limp away.

I moved to intercept him. Big Ben grabbed me around the waist and hauled me towards my car. 'Come on, Hotstuff. I can hear sirens already. Unless you want to waste the whole afternoon explaining things, we need to get moving.'

He had a point. I needed to focus on the case I was

trying to solve, not spend my time earning no money dealing with lowlife criminal scumbags that would probably be out again tomorrow and causing more problems.

Big Ben put me down at my car and ran around to the passenger's side while I fumbled in my bag for my keys again. I slid in and gunned the engine but had to wait for Big Ben while he tried to fold himself into the passenger's seat.

'How do people get into this thing?' he complained, trying now to reverse his bum in first. 'Honestly, it's like getting into a child's toy.'

'I fit in it fine, Ben.'

'Yes, Hotstuff, I can see that.' With a final huff, he settled into the seat. He had his knees either side of his ears.

'Seatbelt,' I prompted.

'You have got to be kidding,' he replied. He was probably right.

'Okay, but you have to travel in the back from now on. You can fit better back there.' Big Ben had been in my car before. That time I had Tempest with me who is a more normal size for a man. Big Ben was like man plus, but I had better not voice that opinion: His ego was inflated enough as it was.

I nailed the accelerator, thrusting the small car forward with Big Ben bracing himself against the side window and the roof. I whipped around the corner, leaving Terrance, Trevor and all their friends behind. I was fairly sure Big Ben was joking about killing some of them. Fairly sure. Nevertheless, I kept going and escaped the Magdalene Estate as quickly as I could.

My House

A few minutes later my pulse had returned to normal. I was driving in traffic, heading into Maidstone and passing Mote Park. A thought occurred to me.

'Benjamin, what were you doing on the Magdalene Estate and where is your car?'

'I wondered when you would get around to asking me that. I was just leaving a young lady's house, and she took me there, so my car is still parked in its garage.'

'Your hook up from last night?' I asked. I was trying to keep the judginess out of my voice but had probably failed.

'No. Goodness, Amanda. My hook up from last night got kicked out this morning so I could go to the gym. Then I met a girl at the gym. She was new and asked me if I could show her around. One thing led to another. She took me home and when I was leaving, I spotted you heading towards your car and figured I could get a lift back into town. When I crossed the road, you were surrounded by chaps who were behaving in a most ungentlemanly manner. I intervened.'

'You certainly did. I owe you one.'

I could feel Big Ben looking at me. I turned my head to look at him. He was grinning at me with a lecherous smile.

'You owe me one?'

'Yes. Benjamin. I owe you a favour in return. It will not be what you are thinking. Honestly, you get so much action, how is it that you don't get bored?'

'Bored? With women?' he said it like the concept was completely alien. 'How do I explain this? I have to assume that you're not a virgin, Hotstuff. And that there is probably more than one man in your back catalogue. Did you notice that each man was different?'

'Well, obviously.'

'What I mean is, their todgers were different. The way they touched you was different. The way they felt was different.'

'Enough,' I implored. 'I don't want to have this conversation.'

'You know, Hotstuff, you're very uptight about sex. For an attractive woman, you seem astonishingly introverted. The point I was making is that every woman is different. They feel different, they taste different. The way they perform certain acts is different. I doubt I could ever get bored exploring the female half of the race.'

I had no answer, about the need to have sex with every woman possible or about my own introverted nature. I was fine talking about sex, just not with men that I don't really know.

'So, what were you doing there?' Big Ben asked, sensing my mood and changing the subject.

'I was on a case. The gentlemen you met were just some local lowlifes.'

If he wanted me to embellish my explanation, he didn't

voice it. The rest of the journey to his apartment by the river took a few minutes. Big Ben wriggled around in his seat until he could extricate himself, thanked me for the lift and waved me off.

I went home. I needed a change of clothes before I considered doing anything else. My bum was damp from rolling in a puddle and my trousers had several dirty marks on them. I might even need a shower to get all the muck out of my hair.

As I came into my apartment block, I walked through a cobweb, the sticky strands getting stuck on my face and hair. The spider had spun it across the doorway that led into the building, but it struck me as odd that no one else had walked into it already today. It was now mid-afternoon. I rubbed at my face and hair until I could no longer feel it, by which time I had reached my apartment door.

Opening the door though, the spider itself abseiled from my hair to dangle in front of my face. I let out a shriek and did a dance to get rid of it, flapping my hands at my hair to make it come loose without wanting to actually touch it. I'm not a fan of spiders.

The offending creature, a house spider with its long legs and tiny body, scuttled away across my floor to vanish under a skirting board just as Bartholomew's words were echoing in my head. That I had walked into a spider's web was nothing more than a coincidence. I was quite certain of that. Nevertheless, I had my eyes peeled for more arachnids as I went through my apartment to my bedroom. Now that I had icky web in my hair, I was definitely getting a shower.

Fifteen minutes later and feeling much cleaner, I was getting dressed between bites of a ham sandwich. In all the excitement of the day, I had forgotten to eat. Thankfully, my fridge usually had something in it that was edible. It was close to half past two and I still had to get to Tonbridge Wells to visit the ghost tours lady and needed to fit in time to sort myself out for tonight's date with Brett.

Standing up from applying a small amount of makeup, I crossed the room to my wardrobe, slipped a pair of low-heeled, tan boots on to compliment the leather jacket I planned to wear, and I was ready. I snagged the plate from the dresser, depositing it in the sink on my way through to my door.

Was that a spider?

In my sink was another spider. Bigger and meatier than the house spider I had encountered before, it was scrambling around for purchase to escape up the stainless-steel walls of my sink but having no luck. It had most likely come up the drainpipe like incey-wincey.

Another spider.

I needed to get rid of it but didn't want to squash it and most certainly had no intention of touching it. I found a cup and a notepad, then berated myself as I ducked back each time it darted towards my hands while I tried to catch it.

I breathed a sigh of relief when I finally suckered it into the cup and dumped it out the window. Again, I assured myself that this was just a coincidence. Nothing to do with Bartholomew at all.

Angry for feeling unnerved, I stuffed my arms into my jacket and went out the door. I had to get to Royal Tonbridge Wells, and it was a good forty-minute drive. Coming back would be worse if I timed it wrong and caught the school-run traffic.

Lily Hallett

I found the ghost tours place easily enough. There were several signs to lead people to their office. It was located just off the main street that ran through Tonbridge Wells and was about one hundred metres from the castle. The town had lots of old buildings, as did many towns and villages in the area and though I had never been on a ghost tour myself, my assumption was that they took small groups around the town and into buildings telling them tales of spectres and ghosts that had been seen over the centuries.

I parked right in front of the office's glass fronted reception area and went to the door. As I pushed it open, a photographer on the other side started taking pictures of me and a tall lady with her hair pinned up came to shake my hand.

'Lily Hallett,' she introduced herself while the photographer took more pictures.

'Amanda Harper,' I replied and handed her my card. She was looking out the window though and not at me.

'Did he travel separately?' she asked.

'I'm sorry?'

'Tempest Michaels. Is he in his own car?' she motioned for the photographer. 'Go outside so you can get his picture as he arrives.'

The photographer scuttled forward and out the door.

'Tempest is not coming, Mrs Hallett.'

'What?'

'He's currently not available. I'm the other detective at the Blue Moon Investigation Agency and will be handling your case.'

'Oh, I'm not sure that will do at all.'

'Why ever not?'

'Well, Tempest is quite famous, you see. All that business recently with the Phantom and the Vampire gave him notoriety in the supernatural community.'

'Is that important?'

'Err, no. No, of course not.' Mrs Hallett was acting strangely.

'Shall we press on then, Mrs Hallett?'

'It's Miss Hallett, or Lily, please. My husband absconded with a younger woman and will not be returning. Come this way please.'

Lily led me through the reception area to a back office. The two rooms appeared to be the entirety of the business premises. Probably the customers gathered in reception before setting off. The poor photographer was still outside waiting for Tempest.

'So, Lily, please tell me what has been happening and what outcome you're hoping to achieve.'

Miss Hallett took her time answering as if she needed to give the question some thought first. Then she led with, 'Are you sure Tempest isn't available? I would really like to meet him.' Realising how rude that sounded, her cheeks coloured. 'Sorry, I don't mean to suggest that you can't do the job quite adequately, of course.'

'Of course,' I replied coolly. 'Tempest is, however, not available.'

'Most disappointing.'

She fell silent again and I had to prompt her once more a few seconds later when I began to wonder if she planned to speak or not. 'The case, Miss Hallett?'

'Oh yes. Yes, of course. Since you're here, we shall have to make the best of it. It's Halloween, so as you might expect, tonight is our busiest night of the year. The whole weekend has been busy in fact. With Halloween falling on a Monday, we have been able to draw our activities out over several days.'

'What is it you wish me to investigate?' I prompted again. I was beginning to tire of Miss Hallett's rambling.

'Yes, I should get to the point, shouldn't I? We have suffered attacks by a real ghost during our tours. It started three weeks ago. On October 12th to be exact. We always have a couple of hidden figures on our tours to jump out and scare the guests. It always goes down well, apart from one time when a lady had a heart attack and we had to halt the tour while the paramedics tended to her. We had to give everyone a refund and…'

I had to interrupt her flow and steer it back onto the subject in question once more. 'You were telling me about the extra ghost.'

'Yes, yes. Well, I was conducting the tour that day myself and there was screaming suddenly when I wasn't expecting it. A young man who was there with his girlfriend claimed that something had touched him. I was polite about it, but I was convinced he was making it up.'

'Then it happened again a few days later, this time a

pair of ladies that were around my age. Gwen was taking that tour, but she was quite shaken when she returned here with the party at the end of their tour. The ladies reported they had been touched by something cold and that it had whispered something to them.'

'What did it say?' I asked. I was making notes and also recording the conversation on my phone.

'They couldn't make it out. It was too faint they said, but it might have been Sir Chelios.'

'Sir Chelios?'

'Yes. He was a knight in the eight century that was murdered by his squire and is said to haunt the grounds of Thornton House. We go through the grounds on every tour. It's just around the corner. I dismissed what they said, but the next night two different ladies said they heard the same thing and that they were touched by something cold.'

I finished writing and looked up. Miss Hallett was looking at me expectantly, waiting for me to ask a question perhaps. Before I could form one, she started speaking again. 'So, should I call the papers?'

'Whatever for?'

'Oh, ah. Never mind then. Will Tempest be back soon? Should we wait until he returns and maybe the two of you can tackle this together?' I was certain she only included me because she knew it would have been rude to tell me she wanted him and had no interest in me. I was curious about what was driving her desire to have Tempest involved.

'Do you have any footage of the tours that might be of use? It says outside that you film every tour.'

'Yes, I guess we do. I hadn't thought of that.'

'I will need to see that footage, please. Can you have it compressed and emailed over to the address on the card I gave you please?'

'Anything else?'

'I really need to speak with the persons that reported being touched and hearing the voice. Can you provide a list of their names and phone numbers please?'

Miss Hallett was beginning to look nervous. About what I had no idea. I was curious enough to ask though, 'You seem on edge, Lily. Is something bothering you?'

'Err, no. Nothing at all.' I was dubious.

Please provide me the list of names and numbers and the footage as soon as you can. I will start analysing it as soon as I can. I will also see if I can find out when Tempest will next be available and if he can accompany me when I return.'

'Oh, that would be super.' Lily beamed. I had no intention of doing that at all, but I had wanted to see how she would react to the suggestion.

I stood up, putting my things back into my bag. I thanked Lily for her time and headed for the door.

The poor photographer, a downtrodden looking man in his late forties was still waiting outside where he'd been instructed to go. I waved goodbye to him as well, slipped into my car and thumbed the ignition.

Then I remembered that I had Brett coming tonight. How could that major fact not have been at the front of my mind? I needed underwear, a wax, and condoms. Well, a wax job was out, just in case I reacted to it. I would do some tidying with a razor instead. The idea of new underwear was enticing, but I considered my bank account and changed my mind. I had a couple of negligees that hadn't seen the light of day for a long while. I could pick one of those. I did need to get condoms though, I would feel much safer going into the evening if I had taken care of that element myself.

I could walk to the shops in Tonbridge Wells from where I was parked, but I didn't wish to linger here in case Miss Hallett had further questions for me. I had spent far too little time investing in myself recently. I reversed from my parking space and spun the little car around. In my rear-view mirror, the photographer was peering through the window now, possibly hoping Lily would see him and let him go back inside.

How Hard Can It Be to Buy Condoms?

MONDAY, OCTOBER 31ST 1547HRS

I had been blithely oblivious of the time until I pulled into traffic and checked the clock on the dashboard. I had more time than I thought. I was caught between the crush of mums on the school run if I headed back to Maidstone now or the crush of workers going home if I waited. I flipped a mental coin and set off.

I didn't really know Tonbridge Wells, so although I was sure I could find a pharmacy and get the product I wanted, I knew where I was going in Maidstone and that seemed easier.

The road to Maidstone was busy but moving, so although it was a bit slow in places, I managed to get home in under an hour. It felt like it had been a long day already. I was fatigued and wanted to spend some time relaxing before Brett arrived, but I had no time to waste. I parked in Fremlin Walk. Boots the Chemist would have what I needed, plus I could run through the lingerie department in the department store that dominated the shopping precinct and see if they had something on sale in my size.

Hustling through the town, I had limited time to complete my tasks before the shops closed so I didn't hang around or allow myself to get distracted by the closing down sale at the shoe shop I had to pass.

Going into Boots the Chemist I realised that it had been so long since I last bought condoms that they had changed the shop around and I couldn't find their new location. I checked my watch. I had been around the shop twice and not spotted them, so I looked for an assistant to ask.

I spotted the familiar white coat the staff in Boots wear one aisle over. 'Excuse me?' I said when I got to him.

He'd been pricing up shampoos and putting them on a shelf but turned to face me now. He was maybe seventeen years old. I was instantly uncomfortable asking him about contraceptives.

'Uh, never mind. Thank you,' I managed as my cheeks flushed. I went to the counter at the front of the shop where a short lady in her sixties was working. 'Hello,' I tried.

'Hello, dear. How may I help you?' she asked, all professional courtesy and good manners.

'I'm looking for condoms, actually. Can you point me in the right direction, please?'

'Oh, whatever do you want those for, my dear?' she said, disdain etched on her face. 'In my day we just used to abstain. Much cheaper too.'

'Erm,' I managed. I hadn't expected to have my sexuality questioned. It was the 21st century for goodness sake.

'Hey, girl, what you up to?' called Patience from behind me. She'd just come into the shop.

My cheeks were still flushing red trying to work out what to say to the shop assistant. Patience flared her eyes at the assistant, grabbed my elbow and pulled me away from the counter. 'Are you buying condoms?' she whispered, trying for once to accommodate my embarrassment. When I nodded, she wheeled me around and led me down the centre aisle of the shop. 'Condoms are this way, Amanda,' she announced loudly so everyone in the shop could hear.

I shot her a look, but she just grinned at me.

'Getting ready for the big date?' she asked.

'Trying to.'

'Did you buy underwear yet?'

'Yes,' I lied.

'No, you didn't, you big fibber. Which is fine if you plan to wear none at all, but don't you be telling me you bought something saucy because I have seen you get undressed before girl and you wear granny pants.'

'No, I don't,' I shot back defensively.

'Girl, do you have on, right now, a pair of slinky, silky panties that a man would want to peel off with his teeth? Or are you wearing the sort of pants you could play sports in?'

I mumbled my answer as we arrived at the small section of shelving that contained birth control products.

'What was that?' she asked, miming that she couldn't hear me, and I needed to speak up. 'Was that: Sorry, Patience, you're right. Please take me to buy underwear next?'

I snatched a packet of condoms from the shelf.

'Not those ones. Don't you know nothing, Amanda? You want these ones.' Patience lifted a box and showed it to me. There was a couple on it, scantily clad and in an embrace. It said featherlight on the label. 'The ones you got are for men with a hair trigger. You don't want those unless you know more about him than you're letting on.'

A woman with two small children hurried them away

with a look at me that suggested Patience and I were two prostitutes discussing oral sex in detail.

'Let's just get them and get out of here.' I placed the box I had picked up back on the shelf, took the ones Patience had and went back to the front of the shop where the tills were located. I selected a self-service till, so I could avoid the opinionated older lady still serving customers but, of course, the product was an age-restricted item, so the till began flashing to draw the attention of a shop assistant to approve the purchase.

The woman had a queue of people to serve so pressed a buzzer to call another assistant over. It was the teenage boy.

'Shopping for yourself?' he asked conversationally as he swiped his pass card to approve the purchase.

Behind me, Patience sniggered as yet again my cheeks coloured.

'Get on with it or lose a kidney,' I hissed quietly. As his eyes widened at the threat, I swiped my card, threw the damned condoms into my handbag and stomped out of the shop.

'That was fun,' Patience chuckled as she joined me in the street. 'So, underwear?' When I didn't respond she pressed me, 'Girl you need to impress that boy of yours. He is fine, maybe too fine to hang out with your skanky, Maidstone living ass even if you're a fine woman.'

She was giving voice to the fears I already had. Brett Barker was wonderful. He was rich, he was handsome, he was brilliantly clever. He could have any woman. How soon before he decided the pretty policewoman was nothing more than that?

'Okay, let's get underwear,' I conceded.

There were shops to suit all budgets in Maidstone, however, Patience pointed out that this wasn't a time to scrimp on money. Now was the time to splurge it on something that would take his breath away. I couldn't fashion an argument.

Two minutes later we were walking through the House of Fraser department store to the lingerie section at the back of ladies' wear. In front of me were mannequins wearing wispy threads of lace and silk and hangers of outfits that were designed to be on the floor seconds after being revealed. The thought made a beeline to my doodah.

'Oh, hold on,' Patience said, stopping so suddenly that I bumped into her.

'What?' I asked. 'Patience, what are you doing?' she was trying to hide behind a mannequin while peeking around it at a woman ten feet away holding up a pair of red panties.

I squealed in surprise as Patience grabbed my jacket and yanked me behind the mannequin with her.

'What are we doing?' I whispered since it was clear we were hiding.

'That's Shaniqua Vincent. She totally stole my baby sister's boyfriend a few years ago. She is a complete whore.'

'Patience is that you?' Shaniqua had spotted us.

Patience cursed. Then she stood up because the mannequin wasn't achieving anything. 'Hey girl, how are you? I haven't seen you in ages.' Patience's face was filled with false enthusiasm.

'Were you hiding back there? You're not still sore about your sister's boyfriend, are you? He was ditching her anyway.'

'Mm-hmm,' Patience replied, her tone guarded.

'So, you in here to buy underwear? They probably have things in your size towards the back.'

'My size?' Patience was squinting at her now. 'What are you saying about my size?'

Shaniqua cocked her hip. One hand on it, one hand still holding the hanger with the red panties. She was the same size and shape as Patience, even her boobs were the same gravity creating dimensions.

'I'm saying you need to look in the big girl section, Patience. It's not like you could fit into these?' she said, holding the panties aloft.

It was like a red rag to a bull.

'Bitch, you're so fat you put on your belt with a boomerang.'

Shaniqua's eyes bugged out and she opened her mouth to retort, but Patience wasn't finished. 'You're so fat it looks like you had a twin, but you ate her. Your ass is so big that George Lucas used it as the trench on the Death Star. Your head's so fat even your eyebrows need to lose weight.'

Shaniqua had heard enough. 'Bitch, you wanna watch your mouth!' She dropped the panties, stepped out of her slut heels and pushed up her sleeves. Then she started taking out her earrings and I knew it was about to go down.

The exchange had drawn the attention of several shoppers who had hurried away and from shop assistants, one of whom had scurried off to find a supervisor. A man in a suit was heading our way.

As Shaniqua advanced, Patience reached into her handbag with one hand then nonchalantly dropped the bag to the floor. In her hand was her police baton; something we are not allowed to carry when not on duty. The man in the suit arrived, but as he opened his mouth to speak, Patience flicked the baton out to full length startling him. Now he was standing next to me with his mouth hanging open.

Thankfully, before I had to step in between them, three security guys from Fremlin Walk ran into the shop. As they ran at Patience, she held up her police ID. I guess she had grabbed that from her bag as well.

'Well done, guys,' she said as they skidded to a halt. 'I caught this one shoplifting.'

'What?' Shaniqua squealed.

'No need to bother with an arrest or taking her to court. The skanky 'ho clearly has no money. Just escort her back outside.' She turned to the man in the suit. 'Good reaction time. Your staff are well trained.' She slapped him on the shoulder. 'Well done. You run a tight ship.'

The poor man's face had no idea what expression it was supposed to show.

As the security guards were trying to get her out of the shop, Shaniqua was loudly protesting her innocence. Patience called for them to stop.

'One last thing. Your face is not a colouring book. Chill with the makeup.'

Shaniqua dove at Patience, a torrent of bad words filling the air. The three security guards had to drag her away while Patience smiled sweetly and waved at her.

'You really should be more careful about who you let in,' she told the man in the suit. 'Oops, time to go.' She grabbed my arm and yanked me toward the lifts.

'I didn't get anything yet,' I protested.

'Then wear nothing. I promise it will be a surprise he will love. We have to go. There are uniforms coming.'

I glanced at the doors. Outside Shaniqua was waving her arms animatedly at the three security guys and there were two police officers with them now. Macey Eldritch and Mark Spence. Just as we vanished from sight where the lifts were in a recess, Macey's gaze followed Shaniqua's pointing arm, and she spotted me. Macey hated Patience, I didn't know why, but she did so Patience was right – we needed to go before they found out she drew her baton.

Halloween

It was full dark out when I returned to my car. On the short drive home, I saw dozens of small children already out with their parents and dressed as pirates or ghosts or witches. It drew a smile from me as I remembered doing the same when I was little. Older kids could be a nuisance. There were always a few that thought it was okay to ruin everyone else's fun by genuinely playing tricks. Most of it was harmless but it was also a day when the police could guarantee someone would utilise the busy streets as an opportunity to commit a crime.

I locked my car and went into my building and up the stairs to my place on the top floor. Big Ben was sitting on my doorstep, his enormous, long legs stretching almost completely to the opposite wall and my neighbour's door.

'Benjamin? What are you doing here?'

'Waiting for you,' he said getting up. 'I got to thinking after you dropped me off, that with Tempest away you would have no one to call upon if you needed a hand with any casework. Then I called Jane, and she said that you were looking into a voodoo case and might need a hand with it.'

'Oh, did she?'

'Yes, she did. She was genuinely concerned that there might be some tangible danger associated with the case.'

I would need to have a word with Jane about empowering women and how we were quite capable of managing without men to chaperone and protect us. Jane was a man underneath the makeup and silk underwear though, so perhaps she didn't really get it.

As Big Ben stepped out of my way, I opened the door with my key and let him follow me inside. In my handbag, my phone started ringing.

It was Kimberly. 'Kimberly. Good evening.'

'He's outside right now. I can see him! I called the police, but they said it was just trick or treaters outside and I should stop worrying.'

'Okay, Kimberly. You're safe enough inside your apartment, right? He can't get in, can he?'

'He uses voodoo magic, Amanda. He can do anything. A locked door is not going to stop him. You need to get me out of here!'

I could hear the panic in her voice. Big Ben could hear it too. The phone was loud enough that her voice was carrying. I thought about it for no more than a second. I had met Bartholomew myself. He was dangerous, I believed that, and he had an entire entourage of followers that could provide him with a false alibi and combine their efforts to make Kimberly's life a misery. Plus, he'd threatened to seek retribution against her for hiring me.

'Kimberly I will be there in ten minutes. Pack a bag.' I

turned to Big Ben. 'Time to make yourself useful. We have a damsel in distress to rescue. Let's go.'

My instruction was moot as he was already out the door and heading toward the stairs. Big Ben liked to be involved, especially if there was a woman in trouble or a chance that he might get to thump someone.

'Is this the voodoo case?' he asked as we got into my car again. This time he folded the front passenger seat forward and climbed into the back seat. There, he was able to lay across the two seats and wrap a seatbelt around his waist.

'Yeah. The client believes she has been cursed by a chap she went on a date with and then rejected.' I went on to tell him about meeting Kimberly last night, about her skin and hair ailments and about meeting both Bartholomew's parents and then the man himself.

'How come you didn't just call the police to his friend's house after they chased you out of it?' It was a sensible question to ask.

'Because they didn't do anything. They were inside their own property, no one assaulted me, even if they were scary as anything. The marijuana could have been present in a quantity that would have warranted an arrest, but equally it might not have been. Because I'm still a police officer for another week and I didn't identify myself as such, and wasn't there as an official undercover officer, any arrest or subsequent prosecution would be thrown out within seconds.'

'The law in this country can be quite messed up,' he observed.

I nodded.

There was very little on the road and I was driving with a heavy right foot, so we arrived on the Magdalene Estate ten minutes after we left my place. It was just after six o'clock according to the clock in my car. There were still kids in costume out collecting candy everywhere I looked. There were adults in costume also, some of them probably the parents of the kids they were escorting, others might be on their way to parties, even though it was a Monday night.

My eyes were darting everywhere, checking for danger, checking for Terrance and Trevor, checking for voodoo priests. All I saw was excited children, holding their mother's hand or running excitedly to the next house. I pulled into the same spot I had parked in last night. I checked all around but there was no one lurking in the shadows that I could see.

Big Ben was getting out anyway, the passenger's seat was already pushed forward so he could extricate his huge frame from my small car.

'What number is she in?' he asked.

'Err, one. On the left, as we go in.' I unclipped my seatbelt.

'Stay here,' he said, putting a hand on my shoulder. He was looking out of the windows and scanning around as I had been. He seemed alert, more switched on than usual. 'Keep the engine running and honk the horn hard if you see anything you don't like.'

'What are you going to do?'

He grinned at me. 'I'm gonna get me a woman.' Then he was gone.

I drummed my fingers on the steering wheel. Yet again I was being rescued by a man. Okay, maybe rescued was stretching things a bit but he'd assumed that as a man he was the best person of the two of us to leave the comfort and warmth of the car and fetch my client.

She was my client, for goodness sake.

Then why was I still sitting in the car? Dammit. I

opened my door, but before I could move, the front door of Kimberly's apartment building opened again as Big Ben came striding through the frame.

Carrying Kimberly.

Dear Lord.

He looked like a Hollywood action hero. He ran down the stairs cradling her like a baby. In his arms, with her petite body, she looked like one. All he needed was a breeze to make his hair flutter and to learn to move in slow-mo. Kimberly had a bag in her arms and was staring at Big Ben with utter adoration. He'd already swept her off her feet.

I shut my door again then leaned across and opened the passenger side. Big Ben upended Kimberly next to the car, patted her bottom cheekily and dived into the back of my car once more. Kimberly's face didn't seem to know what to do with itself. Several emotions were fighting for dominance. In the space of a half-second, I saw fear, excitement, curiosity and sexual horniness.

'Get in, babe,' Big Ben instructed. She almost giggled, but she got in, the door shut, and I got us moving, despite not seeing Bartholomew at any point thus far, I wasn't going to drop my guard. He'd threatened … something. He hadn't said anything that could be used against him. Was that deliberate? Was he clever enough to not expose himself?

I reversed hard out of the parking space, picking up speed then threw the steering wheel around and spun the car through one hundred and eighty degrees. The car snapped around to face the direction I wanted to go, and I was about to mash the pedal but there in front of us was Bartholomew. Flanking him, was a dozen or more of his cronies on either side. All of them were men. All of them were bare-chested and their skin was painted with odd symbols. Bartholomew had white bones painted onto his skin as if his skeleton was superimposed on the outside of his body and he had a large snake of some kind wrapped around his shoulders. Several others were also carrying snakes. They were not armed that I could see but once again, in the light from my headlamps I could see only white where their eyes should be.

Kimberly was hyperventilating in the seat next to me, huge gulps of air that suggested she was going to scream any second. I floored the accelerator and turned hard right. My little car shot across the carpark feeling sluggish with the extra weight in it that I wasn't used to. Bartholomew and his crew were blocking the exit from the building's carpark but there were other ways out.

Between two bushes, I hit the kerbed edge of the carpark and mounted the grass that surrounded the building. We barrelled across the grass, Big Ben swearing from the back seat as I found a large bump in the street and launched all three of us into the air momentarily. Kimberly was bracing herself against the dashboard with one hand while the other was against the ceiling. With nothing holding her bag down, it bounced off her lap and landed on Big Ben. There was another expletive but then I reached the pavement, where I shot across it, narrowly missing a couple out walking their dog and we were back on the road and away.

My word, Bartholomew was scary. No wonder Kimberly had called the firm when the police failed to do anything.

'Everyone okay?' I asked.

Kimberly nodded mutely.

From the backseat, Big Ben swore again. 'I think the middle seatbelt cup went up my arse when you went airborne. Otherwise, I'm just peachy. Shall we go back to yours now?'

Oh no.

With some dread, I realised that I had rescued Kimberly but now had no plan for what to do with her. I wasn't going to be able to convince her to go home. I wouldn't go back there if it was where I lived, and Brett was supposed to be coming to my house tonight. I would have to cancel.

Dammit.

'Are you okay, Amanda?' asked Big Ben from his prone position on the back seat. 'You're muttering to yourself.'

'Oh, err. Just trying to work out what to do with Kimberly.' I briefly considered asking Big Ben if he could put her up for the night. It would mean I could tidy myself up and still have my date with Brett. Before I voiced that idea though, I acknowledged that he would happily say yes but then spend the night pounding her into his mattress. She would go with him because she would feel she had no choice and that would be my fault. I had a responsibility to look after her.

My brain was racing, trying to work out what I might be able to do about Bartholomew. From a legal position, he had still not done anything that would get him arrested. Stalking cases were notoriously hard to prove and often went on for months. I could report his latest escapades, but I needed evidence that he'd perpetrated a more serious crime than standing outside his house with his friends, which is what any defence lawyer would claim. That he was dressed in a scary fashion on Halloween would be laughed out of court.

By the time I arrived back at my building, my pulse had returned to normal, and I had resigned myself to the fact that I was going to have to call Brett and cancel our evening of fun. I was angry about it. The whole evening was planned out in my head, from how I was going to greet him at the door, to how I was going to lead him to my bed and what I was going to do with him then. I had been really looking forward to moving our relationship forward. Plus, a damned good seeing to was long overdue.

Dammit!

Who Sleeps Where?

'Good evening, Amanda,' Brett said as he came onto the phone. His deep voice went right to my Doodah and made my legs feel weak. God, I wanted to feel his weight on me.

'Uh, Brett. Hi,' I mumbled, stammering, and making no sense. 'I, ah. I need to cancel our date tonight.'

'Oh.' If he'd been trying to avoid sounding disappointed, he failed. He didn't say anything else though and a couple of seconds ticked by.

I needed to fill the void in our conversation. 'Sorry. Truly I am. I have gotten myself caught up in a case and had to take a girl in. She will be sleeping on my couch tonight…'

'Understood, Amanda,' he replied, his usual confident, relaxed manner returning. 'It's disappointing, of course, but life is not a linear journey. Will the lady be staying long?'

'Only for the night. I will make alternate arrangements tomorrow.' Even if I had to send her to stay with Patience for a night so I could have Brett visit.

'Shall we reconvene tomorrow?' his voice had that

husky edge again that always appeared when he was talking about intimacy. It was making me feel breathless and horny.

'Tomorrow, yes. Same time?'

'That would work for me. Shall I bring something to drink? A bottle of champagne perhaps? One of the ones you helped me to select in Paris?' I hadn't helped him at all, other than to say that I liked the look of one bottle because it had a cute bunny on the logo. Champagne sounded good though and he only bought the stuff that was so expensive it had no price tag.

'That would be lovely, Brett.'

'I can't tell you how much I'm looking forward to it, Amanda.' We were still calling each other by our first names. I wondered if pet names would follow as so many couples did.

'Me too,' I squeaked, momentarily losing control of my voice in my desire.

I needed to go. Kimberly was already in my apartment with Big Ben waiting for me. I had told them I needed to make a call, then stayed outside to make it. Brett and I said our goodbyes and reluctantly disconnected.

With disappointment ruling my emotions, I pushed my door open and went inside.

Big Ben had found a bottle of wine and had poured Kimberly a large glass, probably to settle her nerves and the two of them were sitting on my three-seater sofa waiting for my return.

'Everything alright?' Big Ben asked. My face probably betrayed my mood.

'Yes. I needed to change my plans for the evening. I had a date arranged.'

Kimberly's head shot around to look at me and then at Big Ben. 'You two are not a couple?'

We both said no simultaneously.

Kimberly was visibly pleased by this news, her body language changing instantly. Somehow, without moving, the distance between her and Big Ben on the sofa reduced. She took a gulp of wine and stared at him. He smiled back at her. No words exchanged but plenty being said.

I rolled my eyes.

'Ben only popped around to check on me actually. We sort of work together. You can go now though Benjamin. I think us girls can handle it from here.'

'What if Bartholomew comes here?' asked Kimberly. 'He might track me here.'

'He can't possibly know where I live.'

'He does voodoo magic. I told you; he can do anything. He probably has a strand of your hair and is performing a tracking spell already. Don't you think Ben should stay with us for a while just to make sure we are safe.'

I thought about the tug I had felt on my hair when I was escaping his house earlier today.

'Kim, we don't need men to make us safe. We can do that for ourselves.' Her attitude was ticking me off, or perhaps I was already ticked off because my plans for this evening had been ruined, but whatever the case, I was displaying impatience.

Kim's face looked upset at my comments. I genuinely thought she might start crying and reminded myself that she was probably a little on edge.

Big Ben spoke before I got a chance, 'We can all just hang out and watch some TV, Amanda. I can stay a while and if any voodoo cronies turn up you will have an extra pair of hands to deal with them.'

'Fine. I need a cup of tea. Anyone else?' I asked over my

shoulder as I walked across the open plan living space to my kitchen.

'Yes, please. White, no sugar,' answered Big Ben.

'I would like more wine. Shall I pop out and get some?' asked Kimberly.

'I'll go,' said Big Ben getting up. 'There is a metro shop around the corner, isn't there?' he asked me. 'Shall I grab a pizza while I'm at it?'

I nodded and waited for him to shut the door. Now that he was out of the house, I took the opportunity to have a quick chat with Kimberly about Big Ben and his social habits.

The kettle was getting agitated behind me as I sat down next to her on the sofa.

'Kimberly.'

'Yes,' she said, turning to meet my eyes.

'About Big Ben.'

'Oh, my God. How are you not sleeping with him? He is so gorgeous. I swear I thought my knickers were going to fall off when he smiled at me. Is he your ex or something? Is it okay if I sleep with him?'

The words had burst out in a torrent as if that was the only thing she was able to think about. I just stared at her, no idea what to say next. I got that Big Ben was attractive. I just wasn't attracted to him. 'Kimberly, I have to warn you that Big Ben sleeps with a different woman every day, sometimes more than one woman in a day.'

'Really?' she breathed out, her voice incredulous and her eyes up and to the right while her brain was sorting the new information. Maybe I had put her off a bit. 'So, he must be really good then. So much experience to call upon and no chance of irritating clinginess afterward, just guilt-free, attachment-free sex. Do you know if everything is in proportion? Because, you know… the rest of him is huge.'

OMG, I really didn't want to think about Big Ben's junk or what size it might be. I rolled my eyes again and got up to make my tea. Behind me, on the sofa, Kimberly was deep in thought.

'Do you mind if I get a shower and change?' she asked. 'I didn't get a chance after I came home from work today.'

'Of course.' I showed her the bathroom and turned the light on.

'I, err. I forgot to pack toiletries in all the excitement.'

'Help yourself to whatever you find.' I couldn't afford expensive shampoos or other items, and my decent perfume was in my bedroom so there jihing she could use that I cared about.

The door closed as I went back to rescue my tea, and the shower came on just as Big Ben came back through the door. I wanted to tell him that he wasn't allowed to shag Kimberly, but I couldn't see how I could stop him since she seemed likely to throw herself at him at some point. I handed him his tea instead and put the wine he bought for Kimberly in the fridge. The pizza went on the kitchen counter from where I flipped the lid open and selected two slices. It was a big pizza.

Presently, Kimberly emerged from the bathroom in a cloud of steam. She was wearing a negligee.

'Do you have a dressing gown or something, Amanda?' she asked. 'I just threw things in from my drawers at home, and this was the only bedwear I grabbed it would seem.' I doubted a tiny, black, silk negligee was the only thing she would have found to wear if it had just been me in the apartment with her.

'Back of the bathroom door,' I answered. I was trying to not be critical.

I had finished my tea and my evening was ruined. I would get rid of Kimberly in the morning. I already had an idea about where to stash her safely. For now, though, I needed to get Big Ben out of my apartment and set up the sofa for Kimberly to sleep on. I was going to take a bath and get to bed.

'Ben, I think we can probably assume that the voodoo lot are not coming to get us now. I'm certain Kimberly and I will be safe without you. I'm sure you're looking forward to getting home.'

'Oh. Well, if you're sure, Amanda. I can hang on if you like. Maybe stay until you're safely asleep.'

'Yes, that sounds like a better plan,' said Kimberly, excitement in her voice.

'No need, Benjamin. This is a safe part of town, and we are in a safe building. I will lock up after you're gone and be quite safe until tomorrow morning.'

So, get out, you big lump of over-sexed meat.

'Okay.' With resignation in his voice, he levered his huge frame off the sofa, wished us both a good evening and went out the door. I locked it behind him. I had been quite worried I would go for a bath and find him shagging Kimberly on my bed when I came out. Knowing Big Ben, he would most likely then encourage me to join them. I felt a lot better now that he was going home.

If Kimberly felt the need to argue she managed to keep her thoughts to herself.

'I'm quite tired, Kim. I'm going to get a bath and get to bed. Please help yourself to any food you find and feel free to use the TV and DVD etcetera. I'll get you some bedding to make up the sofa.'

I went into the bathroom to turn on the taps. There was a spider in it. A big fat one with hairy legs. That was three or more already today which felt like it was more than average. I told myself I was being silly, grabbed the shower attachment and washed it back down the drain hole with cold water. The plug went in, and the hot tap began filling the tub. The quick addition of a bath bomb ensured a relaxing experience.

Thirty minutes later, I was laying in the bath with my eyes closed, wishing I had brought a cold glass of wine with me when I became aware of an odd rhythmic noise coming from my living room. Worried that I already knew what I was hearing, I sat up in the bath and stretched across to open the bathroom door a crack.

There were four feet hanging off the end of my sofa. The back of the sofa faced the bathroom so that was all I could see, but the feet were not stationary, neither was the sofa for that matter as it appeared to be making its way slowly across my carpet. As I watched, Big Ben's hand gripped the top of the sofa for extra purchase.

Big Ben and Kim were having sex on my sofa! FFS!

I almost shouted at them but caught myself and eased the bathroom door closed again. Yelling at them would feel petulant. I might need to clean my sofa though.

I was all done in the bath but didn't feel that I could leave the room and re-enter the main living area with them both naked on my couch. How long would they keep going for? Was Big Ben the sexual tyrannosaurus he constantly claims to be?

Snakes Alive!

My alarm woke me at 0700hrs. The bleeping noise cutting through the dream I was having and banishing it from my memory. I rolled onto my back and stared at the ceiling while I got my bearings. Then I remembered the reason I had set my alarm. I had hidden in my own bathroom for more than an hour while I had waited for Big Ben and Kimberly to grow tired of their nocturnal activities. Then, finally too impatient and uncomfortable to wait any longer, I had hammered on the inside of the bathroom door and announced that I was coming out. I had a towel wrapped around my head which I pulled across my face to shield me from seeing anything I didn't wish to as I speed walked between the bathroom and my bedroom.

It's not that I'm a prude. I just don't want to see Big Ben naked or parts of Big Ben hanging out of the client I was trying to protect.

My question now was whether Big Ben had finished or was still going or had perhaps also just woken up and was about to get started again. I could hear no noise coming from the other side of my bedroom door. Thus, my decision was to get out there quickly before anything could start again.

I threw on some sports gear that I had to hand and opened the door. My eyes were trying to decide whether it was best to take everything in quickly and find out if there was anything I didn't want to see or stare at the carpet until I could verbally confirm if there was or not.

I went with cautious.

'Good morning, Hotstuff.'

I looked up to find Big Ben doing press ups by my front door. He had on his underpants only, there was a light sheen of sweat on his skin and the veins on his shoulders and arms were very visible as they pulsed blood to his demanding muscles.

Kimberly was watching from the couch, as one might watch a chef prepare a meal when you're famished.

'Good morning,' I offered to them both as I crossed the room to the kitchen area and flipped the coffee maker on. I needed it strong and black this morning. There was going to be toast also, a treat to myself. No, bagels! I had bagels in the freezer that toasted up perfectly every time. They were a little naughty, but I was very much in the mood for it.

'Anyone for breakfast?' I asked over my shoulder.

'Yeah, I'm starved,' said Kimberly.

'Benjamin?'

'Probably best if I feed myself. My typical breakfast is a dozen raw eggs with protein powder and veggies, blended and served in three pint-glasses.'

That sounded awful. I took four bagels from my freezer, showed them to Kimberly to gauge her opinion and put them in the toaster just as the coffee machine delivered my wake-up juice.

The toaster popped, the room already filled with the scent of the bagels. I slathered two in butter and handed them to Kimberly. She shuffled across the sofa to make room for me. I eyed it suspiciously. Did it smell? Was it clean? Had anything dripped onto it last night? I went back to the kitchen area and ate my breakfast standing up. I would deal with the sofa later.

Big Ben put on yesterday's clothes. Well, it wasn't as if I could offer him anything fresh to wear. He was going home shortly but stayed for coffee and to ask if there was anything he could do for me. 'I don't think so, Ben,' I said between bites of bagel. 'I will take Kimberly to work and arrange alternate accommodation for her for the next few days until I can crack this case. Today, I will be liaising with the police to determine how best we can deal with Bartholomew.'

'You make it sound all so easy,' Kimberly said.

I cleared my mouth with a swig of coffee. 'There is no mystery to solve really. Bartholomew is the guilty party. Knowing that makes it much easier to find out how he is causing the ill-effects you're suffering. I can make no guarantee, but I think I will have this sewn up and Bartholomew behind bars very soon.'

'Talking about ill effects, I noticed this morning that my scalp wasn't itching the way it had been, and my skin is less red than it was yesterday. Even my teeth feel better. Why do you think that is?' she asked.

I had a theory forming. I needed to check some things out first though. Rather than tell her something that might prove to be false, I instead assured her I would be working on the answer today.

Big Ben was ready to go. He would shower and change and feed himself back at his place. He waited for me and Kimberly to organise ourselves though. I went to my bedroom, Kimberly to the bathroom where we both dressed for the day and sorted out hair and makeup. It took me far less time than Kimberly needed, but a little more than twenty minutes later we were going out of my front door, and I was locking it behind me.

I plipped my car open and got in. Then screamed a scream that people in China must have heard. I propelled myself back out of my car, bounced off a bush and landed in a puddle where I immediately began scrambling away, oblivious to the wet and muck that now covered my favourite tan trousers.

'Um, everything okay?' Big Ben asked. He'd already said goodbye to Kimberly and was walking away as if he hadn't just spent the night riding her like a show pony. His penthouse was a quarter mile away across the other side of the river that flowed through the centre of town.

He was smiling at me in a goofy way. Questioning what could possibly be wrong with me to have elicited such a reaction. I wanted to slap him. Instead, I levered myself off the pavement and pointed to my car.

He could go and look because I sure as heck wasn't going anywhere near it.

He followed my arm and wandered over to my car. 'Oh, yes. I see.'

'What is it?' asked Kimberly as she moved to take a peek. She then screamed just as loud as I had and followed it up with a long string of expletives.

'I'm surprised it bothers you, love,' said Big Ben. 'It's not much bigger than the snake you had to deal with last night.' He was laughing to himself, but I was struggling to find the humour in the situation.

Finding my brave pants finally, I walked back over to my car and peered inside. In the passenger's footwell was the biggest snake I had ever seen. My brain was telling me that it was a Boa Constrictor but was neither sure that I was right nor sure that it mattered. What mattered, was that someone had put an enormous friggin' snake in my car. As I watched, its head came into view, poking up by my gear knob to say hello. Its tongue flicked out sending an involuntary shudder right through my body.

I curse you with spiders and snakes.

Kimberly wouldn't have to worry about her stalker case for long because I was going to kill Bartholomew. There would be prints on the car, hair, and fibre in it. With that, we could nail him. As I pulled out my phone to call the station and get a crime scene team out here, I started to question what we could nail him for. Being sloppy with a snake? It certainly didn't fall into any assault categories. It was stalker behaviour but now it was aimed at me instead of Kimberly.

Nevertheless, I needed to prove his involvement, maybe have another chat with him, but this time do it at his parent's house. With their calming influence, perhaps he would be willing to discuss the recent events like an adult. Or maybe he would just not be willing to pretend he was a voodoo priest with his mother sitting next to him and would thus be forced to answer some of my questions.

Big Ben looked like he was going to get into the car and pet the snake. I grabbed his shoulder and pulled him back. 'Crime scene,' I mouthed as the phone connected at the other end. He got it and gently closed the door of my car using a handkerchief over his fingers to do so.

'So, what now?' asked Kimberly, looking at her watch. 'I need to get to work.'

'I can take you,' Big Ben offered.

I could see no reason for keeping Kimberly with me. I

believed she would be safe enough at work, so I sent her with Big Ben while I waited for the crime scene guys to arrive. They wouldn't take long as they were barely more than a mile away but were not the type that had to react in five seconds ever, so would finish what they were doing before they set off. I went inside to get a cup of coffee and changed my wet clothing while I waited.

Mrs Stone from the floor below me came out of the building as I was going in. She had on her usual combination of pinks to match her dyed pink hair. Mrs Stone was old. Like when she went to school there was no history class kind of old. She was spritely still though despite the years and always gave me the impression she was about to get up to no good.

She smiled at me conspiratorially as we went by each other. 'Someone got some last night, eh? Sounded like your couch was working its way across the whole room,' she cackled.

My face coloured. 'Oh, ah. That wasn't me, actually.'

Now she looked confused. 'Well, what were you doing, keeping an old lady up with all that noise if you weren't getting some?'

'I had a couple of friends stay,' I admitted. That's why it was the couch.

She nodded, smiled inwardly in a way that made me think she was reminiscing about her past, then hurried on her way, shuffling along the path in her house slippers still.

Inside, I brewed coffee and waited by the window. To pass the time I called James to catch him up on recent events and to see what he'd learned.

'Hi, it's James,' he answered helpfully. He'd selected boy clothing this morning. 'How did you get on yesterday?'

I explained about the visit to the Kings house in

Bearsted and my run in with Bartholomew and his gang at the house on the Magdalene Estate. I left out the bit about Terrance and Trevor and about Big Ben shagging Kimberly on my couch.

'How did it go with the ghost tours lady?' he asked.

I had all but forgotten that I had a second case to explore. Bartholomew was keeping me occupied. 'I need to do more research, and I need to go back there and take part in a tour or something, so I can see what is happening for myself.'

'We have an email from Mrs Hallett this morning complaining that they had an interruption last night during their Halloween event. She asked what we propose to do about it. She makes it sound like we should have already solved the case by now and she asked when Tempest would be available.'

This wasn't an unusual attitude. The bit about expecting us to solve the case instantly, not the bit about needing Tempest. I would need to put some more effort into it today. For now, I was grounded though so explained to James about the rather large snake in my car and the curse Bartholomew had supposedly placed upon me.

'I don't like snakes,' James concluded. 'Or spiders for that matter. The little blighters have far too many legs. Hey, I found some information on Bartholomew last night while I was watching Hollyoaks.'

'Tell me.'

'His social profile doesn't tell me much at all, but I liked a load of his friends using a dummy profile I created using a picture of Thea Huntley.'

'The actress?'

'Yup, an old picture before she started getting old and surgery botched her face. Well, I got liked back by half a dozen of the boys so started asking them questions about this and that. I had seven conversations going at one point, then I dropped in that it was Halloween and what were they up to. Three of them said they were practising voodoo with a local priest. One used the name the Magdalene King – does that mean anything to you?'

'Yes, James. It most certainly does.'

'Well, over about an hour I was able to tease out that all the chaps doing voodoo were also working for the Magdalene King. They are all on Bartholomew's social friends' list. But that's not all.'

'Go on.'

'I was asking one guy one piece of information and getting an answer, then asking the next guy a question using the information to make it seem like I already knew what was going on. Then when I got his answer, I would go to the next guy with my next question having gained more detail. What I learned, was that Bartholomew is using Meet Market to pick up girls because he needs one for something. They wouldn't say what it was, I got the impression they didn't know, but it's something big or important and he is getting agitated because he is running out of time.' James finished speaking and fell silent.

What could he need a girl for? His parents said he had a girlfriend. They might have used the word fiancé in fact. Was he just a player and planned to give it all up when he was married? Was the wedding soon? I would need to find out some more about this.

Looking out of my window, I saw a police car arrive and the white van of the crime scene team pull up next to it. Patience Woods got out of the passenger's side of the car dressed in civilian clothes.

'I have to go. The team has come to deal with the snake,' I explained.

'Oh, err, I have more stuff to tell you. About the Meet Market website…'

'I'll have to call you back. Is that okay?'

'Oh. Yes, of course. It might be important. Or might help…'

I was already out the door, four expectant faces staring at me. 'Sorry, James. Gotta go.' I hung up, promising to call back soon to continue our conversation.

'Hi, everyone. There's a snake in my car.'

Patience peered in through the glass of the passenger's window before I could warn her not to. The snake reared its head and came right at her. 'Whoa!' she screamed as she performed what was almost a backflip to get away from my car. 'That's a snake, girl,' she said. Actually, that wasn't what she said, but I can't repeat what she did say because I might have a child one day and I don't want those words to have ever left my mouth.

Brad Hardacre was the other cop in the car with her. He'd been driving because no one who valued their life allowed Patience to get behind the wheel. He strolled across to look in the window as well.

'Hi, Amanda,' he said as he peered in. 'That's a big snake.' It clearly didn't bother him.

'Hello, Brad. How's tricks?'

'Never a dull day,' he replied blithely.

Next to him, the crime scene guys I had called were getting their gear out. I knew them. Their names were Steve and Simon, they were both sweet, older married guys that had no hair and too many kids. At least in their opinion, although I'm certain neither one meant it when they said it. They were taking plastic cases out of the van and placing them on the ground. It had been Simon that answered the phone when I called the extension for their office. He looked across at me now, peering over the top of his glasses.

'What have you got for us, Amanda?' He peered in the car, ushering Brad to get out of his way. 'Python Reticulatus, a large male by the look of him. Not exactly native to Maidstone. Where did you say you found him again?'

'In the car,' I answered. I shuddered again.

'Well, make yourself useful Hardacre, you're not here for your looks. Get animal control please.'

'I already did, professor. They will be here in a few minutes.'

'Jolly good,' he replied, barely acknowledging that Brad was there. Simon had gone into scientist mode. I had seen this many times before. The crime scene guys were all much the same, even the women on the team were cut from the same cloth. The police officers were a handy part of the team, but in their opinion, albeit that they rarely voiced it, they were the brains that got the crimes solved and we were just the monkeys running around finding them crimes to investigate. With nothing to do until animal control arrived, Simon wandered back to the van where he produced a thermos flask and two cups for him and Steve.

I wandered across to talk to them. 'How long do you think this will take?' I asked.

'That depends on several factors, Amanda.'

'I'm listening.'

'We must wait an indeterminate period for the snake to be removed before we can start work. Thereafter, dusting for prints, lifting hair and fibre and anything else we find will take a couple of hours. Were this a murder scene and we were here officially and not just because you asked nicely, it would take all day, but we could be called away at any moment so will be proceeding with the abridged version of our search. You can have your car back around lunchtime, but other than fingerprint results, it will take some time to perform any analysis, and we will need a compelling reason why we would need to.'

I understood what they were telling me. There were too many crimes for the department to waste time analysing evidence from crimes that had no chance of a successful outcome. I would need to show them secondary evidence of Bartholomew's guilt, otherwise, some trace hair and fibre in my car would be dismissed in court as having been passed from my own clothing after my brush with him yesterday.

I thanked them and moved away, wondered what I was going to do with my morning if I didn't have a car. Sitting at home watching daytime TV wouldn't solve any cases or put money in my bank account. An account that relied entirely now on me solving cases.

Patience had recovered from her shock and had come to see what I was up to. 'Sooo, how was last night?' she asked.

I looked at her quizzically, then remembered that she knew I was having Brett come to stay for our first night together and was blissfully unaware that it had all gone south.

'Rubbish,' I replied. I gave her a minute to digest my response, then grinned at her. 'We had to cancel. Remember I told you about the voodoo case?'

'Uh-huh,' she replied suspiciously.

'My client ran into some bother, so I fetched her, and she spent the night on my sofa.'

Patience was squinting her eyes at me. 'Are you sure that was what happened? Are you sure that you didn't just come up with a reason not to have that fine man in your bed?'

I rolled my eyes. Then a thought occurred to me. 'Why

are you here? Did your shift pattern change?' Patience and I were on the same shift pattern, so I would have been due to have been on a night last night and would have been finished about half an hour ago and on my way home. Thus, Patience ought to be on her way home now.

'I was going out the door when I heard about the snake in your car. It was all over the station. Someone asked if it was CI Quinn and Quinn heard them but didn't see who it was, and no one would own up to it – as if anyone would be that daft. So, Quinn messed us around for a while and I was late leaving, and Brad offered me a lift into town because my car is in the shop, and I need to pick it up. Why?'

'It looks like my car is out of action for the next few hours and I need to go places.

Why is your car in the shop?'

'Had a minor collision.' Patience was one of those people that couldn't drive. Somehow, she had passed her driving test first time though and had gone on to pass the police advanced driving exam. Despite this, she hit something with her car at least once a month.

'Can I borrow your car? Just until I get mine back?'

'I have a better idea. I'll come with you,' she said. 'I don't have anything planned for today and I'm not tired, and I have the next three days off.'

'Okay, but I'm driving.'

'It's my car,' she protested.

I fixed her with a look and asked, 'How many times have you crashed this month?'

Her eyes went upwards while she did some basic maths. 'Doesn't matter,' she decided. 'It's still my car.'

'Okay, but if you hit anything. I'm getting out and walking.'

As it turned out, I didn't have to worry about Patience

driving. We left Brad with the crime scene guys just as animal control were turning up. He was unhappy that we were abandoning him to go have fun while he minded my car – his words not mine. Patience and I just waved and blew kisses to annoy him as we walked away. Her car was in a garage about a half mile from my apartment. Down by the river, there were low rent business units, the sort of place that attracts low rent businesses. Patience needed to fix her car so often that she had to go to the low rent, low-cost guys.

Her car wasn't ready though, which caused a heated discussion to ensue. Lots of discussions involving Patience were heated. She's just a fiery woman, and she has a thing about verbally beating men up. When that didn't work, she threatened the man until he gave in and offered her a loan car. He refused to let her drive it though and would only let it go if it was my name on the paperwork as the driver. I guess he'd fixed her car too many times.

The loaner turned out to be his own two-year-old Mercedes E Class. I asked if he was sure he wanted to do this, but he smiled at me lecherously and attempted to peer down my top, making it obvious why I was being entrusted with his expensive car. I was tempted to let Patience drive it anyway. I took the keys, threw him a thank you with a little venom behind it and slid into the plush leather interior.

'Where are we going?' Patience wanted to know. 'I could do with some breakfast.'

'I'm going to the office. James was trying to tell me something earlier and I worry that he is cut off without Tempest here. I don't want him trying to do too much on his own.'

'Hold on. Didn't the office burn down?'

'Not that office. Tempest set everything up in his house

until the place in Rochester can be rebuilt. There will be food there.'

'Where is his house?'

'Finchampstead.'

'Oh. Okay then.' Patience relaxed into her seat. It would take no more than a few minutes to get to Finchampstead, her belly could wait that long. She started playing with the buttons on her chair. She sank toward the floor of the car. Then rose back up again. Then made the seat back fold backward. 'Maybe I should get one of these,' she observed. 'It sure is comfortable. And snazzy. What do you think the monthly payments are on one of these?'

'So much that people would assume you were a prostitute or a drug dealer on the side.'

'How come my mechanic can afford one then?'

'Because you keep giving him all your money.'

'Oh yeah.'

The ride to Finchampstead and Tempest's house took seven minutes. James's little Ford Fiesta was parked on the driveway again. I eased the large black German sedan onto the drive next to it. It barely fit. Tempest's drive always looked big to me. Wide at least but thinking about it know I acknowledged that I only ever saw it with his two-seater sports car and my mini on it.

The front door was unlocked. 'James?' I called out going in. 'It's Amanda and Patience.'

'In here,' his voice echoed back from the dining room/office.

As always, James was hunched over the computer doing something geeky.

'Morning, James. You were trying to tell me something earlier. The police had just turned up with the forensics team to get the snake out of my car,' I said by way of explanation for cutting him off.

'No problem,' he replied getting up. 'I was about to make tea. Would you ladies like some tea?'

'Patience needs some breakfast,' Patience said. At that announcement, her belly gave an audible rumble that sounded like distant thunder.

'Oh, ah. I think Tempest more or less emptied the house of food when he left. There might be something in the freezer,' James replied.

I hadn't thought this through. Patience was eyeing me accusingly. 'You said I could get breakfast here and drove by three different breakfast places to get here.'

'None of them served healthy food, Patience. There is bound to be something here we can make you.' I opened the freezer. 'Look, lots of frozen fruit, vegetables and yoghurt. How about a smoothy?'

'A smoothy?'

James brushed by us to get to the kettle. The debate over what constituted breakfast, and what did not, went on for a while. Patience was very firmly in the camp that felt breakfast had to have some lard in to just to qualify. After a while, I promised to take her for breakfast somewhere when we left Tempest's house.

'So, James. You found out something about Bartholomew trying to pick up girls?' I prompted him to tell me more.

'Yes, his friends suggested that he had some big plan for them, I was playing along and making out like I was in on it all and that got them talking. I started bragging about how cool it was that he cursed them when they wouldn't do as he asked, and I managed to get two names.'

'Names for the girls?'

'That's not all. I then found them on Meet Market by posing as a boy looking for a girl and messaging them using voodoo curse in my message headline.' He'd made three teas already and was talking as he walked us back through the house to the office. He put his tea down and clicked the mouse. 'Martine Davidsdottir and Louise Pemberton have both been on dates with Bartholomew and both broke up with him within a few weeks because he was scary. Both then suffered the same affliction as Kimberly after he showed up at their houses and cursed them.'

'Great work, James. Next you're going to tell me you have addresses for them.'

He reached to the printer and pulled off two sheets of paper. 'Home and work addresses.'

'You also said they referred to him as the Magdalene King.'

'Um, they used the name, but I'm not certain they were referring to him. I printed those pages off as well in case you wanted them.' He juggled some paper on the desk until he found the pages he wanted then handed them over, so I could read them. Patience moved and peered over my shoulder.

We each read the long conversations that James had had with several different men via social media. He'd lulled them carefully into giving away lots of bits of information by doing exactly what he said – he took one piece of information from one person and used it to make it look like he knew something when talking to the next. What stuck out was the use of the name Magdalene King which appeared a dozen times or more. At no point did it say directly that Bartholomew was the Magdalene King, but his last name was King, so it wasn't much of a leap to connect the two.

The Magdalene King. Now that would be a collar.

Patience's belly gave another loud rumble to remind me she wanted breakfast. I wondered if she was able to make it do that on command. I slurped my tea, it was still quite hot, but it was clear that I would have to find food for Patience soon or deal with a whole lot of mood from her.

'James, this is great,' I acknowledged, stuffing the pages into my bag. I will visit the girls this morning, if I can, and see what I can learn.' I finished my tea and walked the empty mug to the kitchen. 'Patience, are you with me?'

'Patience isn't with anyone until she gets fed,' she replied snippily.

'No problem. I will take you to get food now. You do realise though that if we catch the Magdalene King, you will have closed the single biggest case the Maidstone Police Department has ever had.'

Her eyes bugged out. She hadn't been adding things up. With Tempest away, I needed an extra pair of hands. Besides, I was right. All I needed to do was solve the case for the client, Patience could have the arrest. I could see her thinking about it now.

'Well, why didn't you say that to start with? Let's go, girl. We got a bad guy to catch.'

We headed for the door, but James moved to intercept us. 'There was one other thing I needed to tell you.' He had our attention. 'I have a date with Bartholomew tonight.'

Crazy Dates and Safety Words

James had blurted the startling revelation out then stopped talking. Patience and I were just staring at him.

'Say what?' Patience asked.

'I, ah. I went onto Meet Market to create a profile to find the girls Bartholomew had dated and then cursed. Then it occurred to me that if I created another profile as Jane, I might be able to lure him into meeting somewhere. You said he keeps a large entourage with him, but I figured he might not take them on a date, so you would be able to get him alone.' James was wringing his hands together waiting for me to say something, nervous that I might tell him he'd done wrong.

'That's genius,' was what I finally said. And it was. When he dressed as Jane, he was utterly convincing. Apart from the flat chest, it was impossible to tell that it was boy beneath the blonde wig and makeup until he opened his mouth. If you looked close enough you might be able to see his Adam's apple, but he tended to wear large floating scarfs that would cover it up and hang down to cover the lack of breasts.

If we could get Bartholomew alone, we might be able to have a rational conversation with him. Or maybe, if we let the date play out a bit, Jane/James might find out something that would help to close the case – like what it was he wanted a girl for. If his friends were to be believed, he had an ulterior motive that wasn't sex. At least, it didn't sound like it was sex.

'What time is your date?' I asked.

'Eight o'clock at the George in the town centre.' He meant Maidstone town centre. It was a nice bar that used to be a ratty old pub until someone bought it a few years ago, gutted it and transformed it into a wine and gin place. Now it was quite sleek, and because they didn't serve beer at all, the regular crowd of loud, obnoxious boozers avoided it.

'I think we can make this work, but it will need a little planning.'

'You will need to change your outfit for a start,' Patience added unhelpfully. James was wearing black drainpipe jeans and a pair of new looking back sports shoes. On top, he had on a white oxford shirt and a thin jumper. He looked like a man.

'How long does it take to become Jane?' I asked, being cautious about my words as I wasn't sure what he was sensitive about. Was the correct term 'transform'? Or was it regenderfy? I had no idea.

'About half an hour.'

'We should meet before you go so, we can discuss your approach and when we swoop in if it becomes necessary.'

'A safety word,' Patience interjected.

'Safety word?'

'Yes, like when you're doing role play and need to stop it

going too far,' she explained while rolling her eyes at me. 'I always give the boy a safety word so that he can bail out of character if I hurt him too much.' She habitually made me feel like my sex life was boring or juvenile. I sometimes felt like asking her more about it but worried that my ears might start bleeding from the details.

I pressed on, rather than dwell on her role play analogy. 'Shall we say seven o'clock at my place?' I had Brett coming over, but I could push his arrival back a bit and not break the date for the second night in a row. Bartholomew knew my face, so it would be better for James/Jane if I stayed away from the venue. Patience could go though. I would ask her shortly, then convince her if I had to. Tempest often hired in Big Ben and others to bolster numbers when he needed them for a particular case, so I would only be doing the same. It felt like I was operating autonomously and doing exactly what Tempest would do.

'That works for me,' James said. 'I will get changed and come over ready to go.'

'We need to do something about your voice.'

Patience was right. James's voice was a deep rumble from somewhere in his chest. He sounded nothing like a girl. 'Can you make yourself sound like a girl?' I asked.

'I'm not sure,' he replied in a squeaky falsetto. It would need some work. It was a major flaw in our plan if he wasn't allowed to speak. 'I'll work on it,' he said, trying again. The second attempt was as bad as the first.

'Make sure that you do,' said Patience, then turned to me. 'Girl, are we ever getting breakfast?' It's nearly lunch time now.'

'Goodbye ladies,' came a high squeak from behind us as we headed for the door. James sounded more like Mickey Mouse than anything else.

Burgers for Breakfast

Patience's breakfast destination of choice was a burger bar in Aylesford that had been converted from an old petrol station. She was right in that it was closer to lunch than it was breakfast, but she was also right about the food. I had never even noticed the place before and must have driven by it dozens of times. Inside it was full of memorabilia from the fifties and sixties and an old Wurlitzer jukebox was playing tunes from that era. The waitresses were all dressed up with headscarves to hold their fake blonde ringlet hairdos in place and had on hot pants and tight tee shirts. The place was almost full even though it was before noon on a Monday.

I had gone into the place with no intention of eating, but now that I could smell the food, I acknowledged that not only was I hungry, but I also really wanted to try one of the juicy burgers I had seen going by.

We were led to a booth and handed menus to peruse by a woman that was chewing gum and looked like she'd been serving tables for fifty years. 'Have you eaten here before?' I asked Patience. She had already put her menu down and looked ready to order.

'I'm having the double happy burger. What are you having? You should try the buttermilk chicken waffle burger. They served the chicken breast in batter and served between two sticky potato waffles. Not the cheap kind you get in the frozen aisle. These are made here on the premises.' Patience was describing the food with reverent awe.

The waitress came back and there were simply too many options on the menu for me to decide for myself. I followed Patience's advice and ordered the chicken thing. While we waited, I picked up the subject of Jane's date tonight.

'Are you free to go to the George with Jane tonight?' I explained that I couldn't go because of the danger that Bartholomew would spot me, but she seemed less than convinced that this was something she wanted to do. Even the offer of payment did little to sway her.

Then a thought occurred to me, 'Big Ben offered to help out if I needed him on my cases...' I had her attention now. 'Maybe I should ask him to come with you.' I left that idea hanging for a moment. Before she could answer our burgers arrived.

And they looked good.

Patience wasn't touching hers though. Halfway through lifting mine to my mouth I stopped. I realised that Patience was stunned because, despite her claims regarding the matter, she genuinely liked Big Ben. She was in 'like' with him. I doubted she would admit it to me. She might not even admit it to herself, but right this instant she was thinking about the concept of a date with him, and it was sufficient to distract her from the juicy burger that she'd been hankering for just a few moments ago.

I took a bite of mine, 'Eat your burger,' I said around the delicious meat. 'I'll call him when we leave here.' I had misgivings about her seeing him, certainly about her pursuing him as he was basically a dog in permanent heat, but she was a grown woman and could make her own rules.

Patience looked like she wanted to say something. Maybe to deny that she was thinking about him, but instead, she grabbed her burger as if she had only just noticed it was there and took a large bite from it. Grease spilled on her chin.

'So, what's your next move?' she asked once she'd cleared her mouth.

'Jane wasn't able to get a number for the two girls she found via Meet Market, so I'm going to have to track them down physically. I'm willing to bet that they are both at work, so I will try their work addresses first. If I strike out, I can go to their homes tonight.' I took another bite of my chicken burger and snagged a few fries.

Patience finished her burger. I was still only two thirds through mine. She was holding up greasy fingers and looking for a fresh napkin as she'd already killed hers. I passed her mine.

Something tickled my hand, and I looked down to see a tiny spider crawling across it. Instantly icky, I shook my hand to free myself of the creature and sent it flying across to the next table where it landed on a fat sandwich about to go into a man's mouth. Before I could react, he ate it.

Patience saw it too. I averted my gaze in case anyone else had seen. It wasn't like I had done it deliberately. Then the man started choking. He was in his sixties and badly overweight, his stick-thin wife opposite him, nibbling at her own sandwich, now looking at him with a worried expression as he was clearly not able to breathe.

He was making gagging noises as he tried to do something about the blockage in his throat but was getting nowhere and starting to change colour. All around him people were looking his way but doing nothing.

'Heimlich.' I cried as I sprung from my chair. 'Sir, I need you to stand up.' Tugging at his sleeve got his attention. I couldn't get behind him as he was wedged into a booth, so I had to get him out to get my arms around him.

He weighed a ton and was barely supporting his own weight by the time I managed to get my fists into his ribcage and heave. A colossal chunk of meat was ejected from his throat to land in his wife's lap. As he started to breathe again, a round of applause rippled about the room and the manager, who had just arrived at our table, shook my hand and thanked me for my first aid skills. Our meal was on the house it seemed.

At our table, Patience was white as a sheet, her mouth hanging open in horror. 'That spider was meant for you,' she squeaked.

I stayed with the man until I was sure he was okay. When he went back to eating his sandwich, I decided he probably was. Ten minutes later we were back in the car and heading for the business district of Kings Hill.

'That spider was sent to kill you,' Patience said.

'What? How does a spider get sent to kill someone?'

'I saw it on an old James Bond film. The one with Roger Moore and all the voodoo. They send a snake or something to get him. The snake is under the voodoo priest's control, so it does what he tells it.'

'Patience it was just a little spider.'

'So why did the man instantly choke on it?'

'He choked on his sandwich.' I was trying to keep my voice calm in contrast to hers which was bouncing around like the world was going to end any moment. 'The spider was a coincidence, nothing more.'

We lapsed into silence as I turned the car onto the West Malling bypass heading West away from Maidstone.

The work address for Louise Pemberton was in the business district there where I knew many large firms housed their national HQs. The purpose-built, and very nicely landscaped layout provided lots of parking and large low-rise office buildings that wowed customers without the firm needing to worry about managing their own facility. I knew all this because I had gone there with others to arrest people several times and had once sat waiting with a secretary that had told me all about it.

Louise worked for a firm that made carpets. Not that they had any in the office where she worked, the office was for administrative functions such as HR and accounting. A pleasant, middle-aged lady in the reception area asked us if we had an appointment.

'No, ma'am,' I answered. 'We are private investigators. I have just a couple of questions for Louise if she can spare us a few minutes.'

The lady picked up her phone to call through to her. 'Please tell her this is pertaining to Bartholomew King,' I advised, hoping that would get her attention.

We sat to wait on expensive-looking chrome and leather chairs. However, a young lady came into reception from the office area less than a minute later looking for us. She was tall and blonde with some Asian heritage showing around her eyes.

I stood up to introduce myself and hand her a card. 'Amanda Harper, thank you for seeing us. This is my colleague, Patience Woods.'

'This is about Bartholomew?' she asked. I nodded, and

she invited us through to a breakout area in the corner of their plush open-plan office.

'I'll try not to take up too much of your time, Louise. My client recently met with Bartholomew via a dating website, but when she rejected him after a first date, he pretended to curse her with a voodoo spell.'

'Let me guess: Her hair began to fall out and her teeth and gums bled, that sort of thing?'

'Exactly right.'

'The same thing happened to me. I met him on Meet Market about two months ago. He was handsome and charming to talk to over the internet, but face to face he was just creepy after a while. We went on three dates and when I ended it on the third date by politely saying I didn't wish to see him anymore, that I felt we were incompatible, he went nuts. We were in a restaurant, and he blew some kind of weird grey powder at me. He put his hand in his pocket, did some odd chant thing then blew into his hand and out came all this fine ash or something. He told me I was cursed to be ugly and that the curse would remain in place until I changed my mind. I haven't been on a date with anyone since.'

'Did you suffer any symptoms? Hair falling out that sort of thing?'

'Yes, hair loss, gums bleeding, a sudden outbreak of spots. It freaked me out for a while, and I thought that I was seeing him. Bartholomew, I mean. I would spot him from my car on the way to work, just staring at me from a pedestrian crossing or he would be in the supermarket on my way home like he was there by coincidence. He didn't approach me ever. I felt that he was waiting for me to approach him to beg forgiveness, so he would lift the curse or something.'

'Your hair and skin look fine now. What happened?'

'I took a week off and went to stay with my gran in Scarborough. I thought that he would get bored of stalking me if he couldn't find me. I also went to a chemist and asked them about the problems I was having and got a whole new range of toiletries that were free of perfume and other additives. The Free From range. Have you heard of it?'

I nodded that I had.

'Well, it cleared all the problems up within two days. I returned after a week away and haven't seen Bartholomew King since and hadn't heard his name nor given him any thought until you arrived today.'

'Do you think you were cursed?' Patience asked.

'I don't know what to think,' Louise answered. 'It seems like nonsense, but he puts on a convincing act.'

Beside me, Patience was all but hyperventilating. 'Is your friend alright?' Louise asked. The answer to that would depend on what we were comparing her to. I ignored her and moved on.

Louise had nothing much more to tell us and I had a theory that this went some way to confirm. I elected to leave the second lady, for now, I had more pressing lines of enquiry to pursue and felt it likely that her tale would very much resemble Louise's.

Heading back down the bypass to the motorway, I asked Patience if she was doing okay.

'Not really. I think I should go for a lie-down,' she replied.

'Patience this isn't really voodoo. It's just clever tricks and some luck. He is relying on people's superstition to make it seem real.'

'Girl, you got cursed with spiders and snakes and now they are everywhere and trying to kill you. Those other girls got cursed with ugly and their hair fell out. It all seems pretty friggin' real to me. When your hip or shoulder or back starts hurting later – that's going to be him sticking pins in a voodoo doll. Patience has had enough. Patience wants to go home.'

'I thought you were going to help me catch the Magdalene King and get the biggest bust ever.'

'Not if it gets me cursed, I'm not.'

'How about if I prove how he's doing it? I'm taking you back to Kimberly's house, so we can check something there.'

'What?' she asked.

'Her toiletries. Bartholomew is a chemist. He got a double first at Oxford and his parents are both chemists. If I wanted to make a person's hair fall out, how would I achieve that?'

'Cast a voodoo spell?' she hazarded.

'Or perhaps just put something into her shampoo that would make it fall out all by itself. Same thing with her teeth and gums and the same thing with her skin. I need to get all the toiletries from her house and get the crime scene guys to check them for me.'

Kimberly's House

Patience was tired from her shift and wanted me to drop her at her house on my way to Kimberly's. It wasn't much of a detour. Once I had done so, I called Big Ben.

'Hotstuff,' he answered.

'Benjamin,' I replied, resignation in my voice because he was going to keep calling me Hotstuff or toots or something until I gave up and accepted it. 'Are you available tonight? I need you for a stakeout in a bar.'

'What time and will there be girls there? Forget I asked. If I go there, girls will arrive shortly afterward.'

I rolled my eyes. 'Actually, Patience is going. We are tailing the voodoo guy, and he knows what I look like so I can't go. Patience was a little reluctant but the two of you will just look like you're on a date. It's in the George.'

'Patience, huh. Still trying to get a second bite at the cherry.'

'Well, she will be clocking hours for the business the same as you so don't worry about it. She will be there to work.'

'How do you know he will be there?' Fair question.

'He has a date with Jane.' At the other end of the phone, I heard spluttering.

'You made me choke on my tea. For a second I thought you meant Tempest's assistant.'

'I do. Jane set herself up on a dating website and now has a date with him tonight.'

'Is she planning to use hand signals? She looks convincing but there is no disguising her voice.'

'Yeah, I'm a little worried about that myself. She might have to pretend she is mute or something.'

'Well, it's going to be entertaining if nothing else. I'm in.'

'Jane is meeting him there at eight o'clock and we are meeting at mine at seven to go through planning and emergency escape if necessary.'

'Seven at yours. See you then.'

We disconnected just as I was pulling up outside Kimberly's place. I looked around to see if Terrance and Trevor were anywhere in sight. They were not, and I was in a different car, so I hoped I would be able to get in and out without another showdown.

I had taken a key from Kimberly last night just I case I needed it for anything and to make sure that she wasn't tempted to go back there for anything she might decide she couldn't do without.

Walking up the path to her building, I saw that a window was open in what I judged would be her bedroom. She must have forgotten to shut it. I let myself in through her front door then froze. I could hear movement coming from somewhere inside the flat.

I crept forward into the central living area. It was open plan like mine but there was no sign of life. Then a man in a balaclava walked out of her bathroom. There was a half second when we just stared at each other, then my phone rang in my bag and like it was a starting gun, we both burst into action simultaneously. More from habit than anything else I yelled a police instruction to stop. Pretty much like everyone else that heard the instruction to stop, he just kept on going. He hurdled the couch, bolting for the bedroom and was out the window before I got anywhere near him. He was slick and fast. I followed him out the same window, dropped to the dirt and ran in the direction I had seen him disappear. The Magdalene Estate was a rabbit warren of pathways and alleyways that he knew better than me. I lost him no sooner than I attempted to give chase.

Out of breath from the sudden adrenalin and exertion, I staggered back to Kimberly's flat. I had left the door open, which I now shut, and had thrown my handbag somewhere when I rushed after Bartholomew. I needed my phone so that I could call this in. I couldn't identify the man, but I was certain it was Bartholomew.

My bag had skidded under a coffee table and wasn't visible which gave rise to a brief flutter of panic when I couldn't find it and worried it had been stolen. The missed call was from the forensics lab. I called him back.

It was Steve who answered. 'Forensics.'

'Steve, it's Amanda. I have a missed call from the lab.'

'Oh, Hi, Amanda. We've finished with your car. It's still outside your house.'

'Oh, good. I have another job for you though. I'm at a client's house. I think the same man that put a snake in my car also broke in here. I need you to test the chemical composition of some toiletries. Can you do that?'

'Can we? Well, yes. It's what we do. But we are rather backed up currently. How soon do you need results?'

'This evening?' I asked hopefully.

'Ha!' he scoffed. 'Look, Amanda, if you can bring the things you want me to check, I will do what I can, but if you need us to come to you, I will lose more time.'

I thought about it. I really wanted to have this place swept for prints. 'Will you be able to lift prints from shampoo bottles and that sort of thing?'

'Probably yes.'

'Okay then. I will be with you in half an hour.'

'Super. By then I should have your fingerprints from this morning checked. If they are in the database, we will be able to ID them.'

I went through to Kimberly's bedroom to shut the window before I forgot to do so, then went around the house making sure everything was secure. I wasn't carrying any evidence bags but in her kitchen drawers, I found a roll of freezer bags. Using sausage tongs from another drawer I carefully took all her toiletries and packed each one into a different bag. I had twenty-six bags when I was done.

I put them all into two carrier bags I found stuffed into a box in a utility cupboard then locked up once more as I left.

Had I seen Bartholomew King? Was he the Magdalene King? Maybe. I needed to speak with CI Quinn.

Maidstone Police Station

True to his word, Simon had the fingerprints analysed by the time I got there. Unfortunately, they were all mine.

'Most of the prints we lifted were partials and from the driver's side. Around the door handle and places where one might expect to get a print, they were mostly smudged.'

'Like you would get if the person last using the door handle was wearing gloves.'

'Exactly.'

Simon wandered over to join us. 'What's in the bags?' he asked.

I held them up. 'Twenty-six different toiletry products that I believe may have been tampered with.' I explained about the case I was investigating and my theory about Bartholomew putting something in her shampoo to make her hair fall out and something in her toothpaste to make her gums bleed.

They both nodded then Simon held out his hands to take the bags from me.

'The lady wants answers today.' Steve pointed out.

'Ha!' scoffed Simon. 'Fat chance of that.'

'Can you just do a fingerprint check on one bottle for me?' Simon's expression was pained. He wanted to say no, but I could see he was wrestling with saying yes. 'Please,' I added with a lot of sugar on it.

'Dammit,' he swore. 'Okay, but just because it's you. Which bottle?'

I had taken some from inside her shower as those would be the ones in current use. I had then emptied all other toiletries from the cabinets above and below the sink for good measure. I looked through the bag until I spotted the right one, it was a cheap supermarket brand and mostly empty. The bottle had been dry to the touch though because Kimberly hadn't used it in more than a day. If the intruder had touched it, his fingerprints would still be on it.

'Well, it won't take me a moment to just check this one,' Simon admitted. The old dusting for prints method was long gone in the modern lab. Now they pass a scanner over the object, and it reads the prints off instantly. Of course, I have no idea how it works, and everyone still says they are dusting for prints when they perform the task.

Less than a minute later the three of us were crowded around a screen watching the symbol on it rotate while it spooled information. It was comparing the fingerprints it had found to the National database. It was instantaneous in theory, but it still had millions of records to check.

The computer beeped and there was Bartholomew. His record from the alleged stalking case meant his prints were forever in the system.

'Harper, what are you doing here again?' CI Quinn's terse voice cut through the quiet air of the lab and ruined my moment. 'Why is she here?' he then asked Simon and Steve, essentially dismissing me.

'Well…'

CI Quinn cut Simon off the second he started speaking. 'Have you completed the work on the Hopkin's murder yet?' He was utterly calm as always. Annoyingly so.

'I did say that it would take a lot of hours to get through all the…'

Ci Quinn cut him off again. 'Then why are you wasting time with Miss Harper.' He hit the Miss extra hard to make sure I noticed. In his eyes, I was already a civilian. I could hardly argue against his point, but he didn't need to be such a dick about it.

I was starting to feel bad about sweet-talking the guys into helping me. When Quinn next opened his mouth, I cut him off. If I was a Miss now, he had no further rank or power over me.

'What I want you both to d…'

'Hey, Quinn! Shut up for a second.'

He looked stunned. Like I had slapped him. 'If you give these chaps a little leverage, they may just deliver you the Magdalene King.'

He'd been about to shout something back at me when I said the name I knew he would pay attention to. CI Quinn was all about career. He wanted the big busts. He wanted the limelight and went after it at the expense of lesser cases where the victims got no justice. He'd been after the Magdalene King for years. No one could prove he existed, but someone was peddling drugs in the area and everyone that ever got busted said they worked for the Magdalene King and then never said another word.

It could all just be a legend, but CI Quinn didn't think so. I had his attention. 'My latest client has been targeted by a man that has been referred to by others as the Magdalene King. The voodoo link is there; I have witnessed it for myself. He has a large following and he is a chemist, so the drug connection is also present. I need more time to gather evidence, but this is a great lead.'

'A great lead,' he repeated slowly. 'How would you know to define such a thing?' and there was the old CI Quinn back. 'Show me what you have,' he demanded.

I went into a deeper description of what I knew. However, as I was talking, I realised how thin my case against Bartholomew was. Not only that, all the evidence that pointed towards him being the Magdalene King was highly circumstantial.

'This is the man?' Quinn asked, pushing between Simon and me to look at the screen. 'Huh.' He snorted. 'Harper the Magdalene King case was opened almost thirty years ago. This man looks barely twenty.'

'Is it not possible that the title has been handed down or even that what started out as a legend has become real because someone, Bartholomew, assumed the role.'

He stood back and put some space between himself and the rest of us. He was rubbing his forehead in a bored or disappointed manner. 'Harper, I want you to listen to what I have to say and to believe that I'm saying it for your own good. You were never any good as a police officer. When you decided it was time to move, I was pleased for you because you were never going to succeed in uniform, but the role you have moved to is worse. Working for that char-latan Tempest Michaels with his ridiculous paranormal cases. You have no investigative skills with which to solve his cases, but no doubt he hired you for your looks rather than any other attribute.'

'Are you quite finished?' I asked between gritted teeth.

'No, Harper, I haven't. You need to leave the detective work to those with some ability for it. Recognise that you're wasting your time chasing around after criminals or, in your case, fake ghosts, and find something that you can actually do.'

'Such as?' I really wanted to hear what he had to say next.

'Have you thought about the retail sector?' I was seriously considering kicking him in the nuts. 'I can see that I'm not getting through to you, so I will make it easier for us all. You're banned from the station. I don't expect to see you here again unless you're handing over your ID card and uniform. As for you two,' he addressed Steve and Simon. 'If I catch you processing her rubbish, I'll have your wages docked.'

I was raging inside, but I was trying to emulate his calm exterior, the one that never got ruffled. 'Are you going to ignore my leads on the Magdalene King case?'

This time he laughed. 'Harper you have no leads. Have you not heard a word I was saying? You don't know what you're doing. Now get out and give up this foolish game.' Then he turned and went, only he didn't go at all. He merely went to the door to hold it open for me.

I glanced at Steve and Simon, whispered an apology for dropping them in it and I left. I couldn't think of anything else I could do. But I wasn't leaving it there. Not on your life. I was going to solve this case and the next one and the next one and even though I knew that CI Quinn would never acknowledge my success, I would know that he'd always been wrong. Caring about his opinion was beneath me, that was what I was telling myself as he had one of my former colleagues escort me out of the station.

Arresting Bartholomew

With Bartholomew's fingerprints on the shampoo bottle, I had probable cause for arrest. I could place him in the victim's house. He was wearing a balaclava, so I couldn't identify him as the man who fled, but I was going to arrest him anyway. To hell with CI Quinn, let's see how Bartholomew holds up under some questioning.

I called Patience.

'Hey, what's up, girl?' At least she was awake.

'I need you to come with me to arrest someone. I can place Bartholomew King in Kimberly's house. I have his fingerprints on her shampoo bottle. I think he was tampering with it.' What I most needed was to have the lab guys work out what was in the shampoo or toothpaste, so I could prove my hunch was right. That avenue was closed off to me now though so later I would need to rescue Kimberly's toiletries and take them somewhere else for analysis. Unfortunately, that would cost money, but it felt necessary.

'Amanda, I don't want to mess with no voodoo priest. What if he curses me?'

'Patience it's not voodoo. There are no curses being levied. He is just a clever man using trickery to fool people. His only weapon is superstition. He uses it against people like you. I'm going to drop the loan car off, get my car from my place and will pick you up in half an hour. Put your uniform on.' It was best when dealing with Patience to give her no option.

'Aren't you all Miss Business today. What if I don't want to? What if Patience has other things to do with her Tuesday afternoon?'

'If you do this, I will make sure that Big Ben breaks his once only rule for you.' I had no idea how to make him do such a thing, but I also knew that I had her now.

'Dammit, girl. Why didn't you just start with that? I'll see you in thirty.' She hung up.

Thirty minutes later I was pulling up outside her building. Her mechanic had been just as lecherous the second time, grinning and chewing gum while not even trying to make contact with my eyes. I threw the keys at him and power-walked back to my place. I debated going inside to change into my uniform, but it seemed just as easy to change at Patience's place. I had never thought I would put it on again, but here I was carrying it into her place.

Patience opened the door as I got to it. 'I saw you coming. Does your car smell like snake?'

'What does a snake smell of?' I asked as I laid out the uniform and started getting undressed. Patience was already in her gear.

'Huh. Good question.'

'The car looks the same as always, but I do want to get it

valeted none the less.' As I tied the laces on my boots, Patience asked what we were doing.

'We are going to his house in Bearsted to speak with his parents. If we get lucky, he will be there, and we can just arrest him. If he is not, I intend to have his parents tell me where he is. Once he is in custody, and away from the security of his friends, I expect he will stop his ridiculous pretence and answer my questions. Maybe he will even admit to spiking Kimberly's toiletries. The aim is to stop him from stalking her, but if I can provide proof that he has caused her harm she can pursue a civil case against him and seek compensation. The family certainly have the money, and I think she deserves it.'

'Okay,' Patience replied as I stood up and checked everything was in place. 'But if I see one voodoo doll, you're on your own.'

The drive to Bearsted took nineteen minutes from Patience's place. Traffic was slow due to school-run mums clogging the roads. I parked right in front of the house again, but this time, through the fence I could see the same flash Japanese car that had been outside Mason's house yesterday. On the way, I had called Brad Hardacre, confirmed he was out in a squad car and had him come to our location.

I rang the doorbell and waited for it to be answered. I had described the house and Bartholomew's parents to Patience on the way over. She was standing back from the front door taking the property in now though, looking around appreciatively.

'I wish I had paid attention in chemistry class,' she said. 'Why couldn't the teacher just have said that I could have this if I just learned the boring crap he was saying. I would have done my homework then instead of watching cartoons.'

I heard a noise behind the door just before it opened. This time it was Mr King senior in the open doorway. The jovial, convivial expression he'd greeted me with last time was still there in the background but losing its battle for dominance with annoyance because there were now two police officers on his doorstep.

'Is your son here, Mr King?' I asked, not giving anything away.

'Yes. He arrived home just a few minutes ago.'

'Can you take me to him, please?'

'I must insist you tell me why you wish to see him first.'

Patience came to stand by my right shoulder. 'We have evidence that places him inside the property of Kimberly Kousins, the woman I came to see you about yesterday. Her claim against your son has been substantiated by physical evidence and further evidence is being analysed at this moment. It will greatly help your son's defence if he willingly accompanies us to the station.'

'Who is it, dear?' asked Mrs King, appearing by his side. 'Amanda is that you? Surely, you're not back here to bother Bartholomew again?'

'I'm afraid I am, Mrs King.'

'They claim to have evidence that he was stalking the young lady she told us about yesterday.'

'I can't believe that,' she replied.

'Nevertheless, I can assure you it's true.'

'He isn't here,' she lied, which came as surprise.

'Your husband said that he had just arrived home,' I replied, making it clear that I didn't believe her.

Just then I heard a door slam deep within the house and

seconds later the sound of footsteps running across the gravel around the side of the house.

The car!

Patience was already running, I followed, rounding the side of the house a few paces behind her. Ahead of us, by his car, Bartholomew was fumbling in his pockets for his keys. He pulled them triumphantly from his back trouser pocket and checked where we were just in time to see that he was too late. Patience barrelled into him, knocking him to the gravel.

'Bartholomew King I'm placing you under arrest for the crimes of harassment and of breaking and entering. You do not have to say anything, but it may harm your defence if you do not mention when questioned something which you later rely on in court. Anything you do say may be given in evidence.' I finished the caution just as Patience was ratcheting the cuffs onto his wrists.

'Oh dear. This is most unfortunate,' said Mr King.

'Will you be alright, Barty?' asked his mum.

'Your son is under arrest, Mrs King.' I wanted to add that this could have been avoided if they had helped more yesterday but I wondered if they even knew what he was up to. 'He will be taken to Maidstone Police Station and processed, where after he will be questioned in connection with several crimes.'

In the road, Brad pulled up in the squad car.

'Young lady,' Mr King calmly addressed Patience as she hauled Bartholomew off the ground. 'You're a woman of colour, just like us. How is it that you dare to turn against us? This is not acceptable behaviour.' Mr and Mrs King are literally the calmest, nicest people on the planet.

'Sir, I suggest you move out of my way so that I don't have to arrest you for obstruction.' Patience was also being remarkably calm, normally she would have roughed Bartholomew up a bit in taking him down and would have given Mr King a mouthful. Perhaps it was the calm demeanour that Mr King projected.

'This will not be forgotten,' he warned.

'That sounded like a threat.' Patience thrust Bartholomew into the back of my car and shut the door. 'Was that a threat, Mr King?' she asked turning back to face him.

He remained silent, just staring at her.

'Let's go.' I grabbed the sleeve of her uniform and tugged her back towards the street. I didn't think it had been a threat, but I also didn't know what he meant.

Brad was waiting by the car with Robbie Fischer, a new guy that was twenty-two but looked more like seventeen.

'Brad, can you follow us back to the station in my car?'

'Err, sure,' he said. 'Everything okay? Didn't you hand your uniform back already?'

'I didn't get the chance yet. I guess this will be my last arrest though.'

He nodded. 'Come on, Robbie.' I threw him my keys.

We left Bearsted with Bartholomew in the back of the squad car. Before we had gone around the first corner he started talking.

'You're far in deeper trouble now than you can possibly understand.'

'Are you threatening a police officer, Mr King? Patience, please takes note of what he is saying.'

Patience pulled out her issue notebook, but Bartholomew carried on as if I hadn't spoken.

'How are you enjoying the snakes and spiders? There is no hiding from my curse. It will find you wherever you go. This latest insult though deserves some special treatment, I think. I shall leave that as a surprise though. Not so for you, I'm afraid,' he said, turning his head to address Patience. 'My father was right. You have betrayed your own people. I shall make you my slave for that.'

'What?' Patience squealed. 'Your gonna make me your what? Boy, you ought to know better than to use the S word around other black people. What is wrong with you?'

'You will not have to wait long. The ceremony is planned for Friday night.'

'Huh? What ceremony?' I asked.

He clammed up then. Refusing to say another word. The remainder of the journey to the station was conducted in silence.

I dropped Patience and Bartholomew off and parked the car. By the time I had made my way through the station, she was already at the front desk with him getting ready to hand him over to the duty Sergeant for processing. In less than thirty minutes, I would have him in an interview room and be able to show him the evidence that proved he'd been inside Kimberly's house.

'Harper!'

'Oh, nuts.' I cringed and swore under my breath.

Quinn's shout had caused the entire room to go silent.

'Harper, what the hell are you doing in uniform again? Take it off and get out.' He was storming across the room, his face incandescent with rage. 'Woods. I might have known you would be involved as well.'

He was staring down at both of us, once again holding all the cards.

'Why is this man in restraints?'

'Sir he …'

'Be quiet, Harper. I was asking the police officer.' He

didn't even look at me when he said it. He was staring at Patience.

'Well, um. He ran when we went to arrest him,' she managed, her voice betraying how unsure she was.

'What cause did you have to arrest him, Woods?'

'Well, um.'

'His fingerprints were found inside the house of a woman that has reported him to be stalking her,' I said quickly before he could silence me again.

'I told you to be quiet. Since you insist on talking and believe you know how best to proceed, why don't you tell me why you think that gives you grounds for arrest?'

I was confused now. I could place him inside the property. He had no right to be there. It was an open and shut case.

'Struggling for an answer, Harper?'

'No, I.'

'Enough. The person you have arrested was in a relationship with the supposed victim, yes?'

'They went on one date.'

'So she claims. I have had the family lawyer on the phone. He claims that Mr King has been involved in a long-term relationship with Miss Kousins. His fingerprints will be all over her apartment. Anything else, Harper? A shred of evidence that you could use to justify arresting this man?'

My mind was racing. I could feel the earth shifting beneath me like it was tipping and threatening to throw me off.

'I thought not,' he concluded. 'Takes this man's cuffs off.' He indicated to the desk Sergeant who scurried across the silent room to perform the task.

'Your police ID, Harper,' he demanded. Then hissed, 'Now,' when I failed to instantly react.

Reluctantly, and with half my former colleagues watching, I took out my ID and handed it to him. He snatched it from my grasp. 'Now take that uniform off and hand it in.'

'I don't have a change of clothes with me.'

'I don't care, Harper. Just get it done.' He dismissed me and turned to Patience. 'Go and wait in my office, Woods.' Then he walked away.

I felt like crying. I could feel my face puffing up from the effort of holding the tears back. He was such an arse.

I was bumped then as Bartholomew pushed past me. 'Enjoy the spiders, won't you?' he said, then tapped Patience on her shoulder as she was trudging towards Quinn's office.

'Don't be pushing your luck today, Mr King.'

'Just remember what I said please. It will happen soon enough.' I could see Patience wanted to react. He was goading her, but we had both just been publicly admonished in front of him and he knew he could do whatever he wanted in this moment. 'I wish I could stay and entertain you for longer, ladies, but I have a date tonight.' He waved us goodbye and went out the door.

I had been lying about not having a change of clothes. It was in my car, so I retrieved it, went into the changing room and took the uniform off for what I was quite certain now would be the last time. The tears that had been threatening finally came now that I was on my own.

Administration

When I was finally dressed in my own clothes and had composed myself again, I fetched the other sets of uniform from my car and went to hand them in. I was made to wait, which gave me even more time to stew. I had hoped I would see Patience. I had dropped her in it. Unlike me, she still had to put up with Quinn. I could leave here today and never deal with him again. Or if I did, the next time I saw him he wouldn't have the advantage of rank to hold over me.

I kicked the wall. It didn't make me feel any better and I hurt my toes.

My phone rang. I pulled it from my bag to see that it was Kimberly calling. I had completely forgotten about her.

'Hi, Kimberly.'

'Yeah, hi, Amanda. Um, I finished work and came outside to go home and then remembered that I don't have anywhere to live right now. Do I come back to your place?'

'Sorry, Kimberly. I should have given this more consideration.' I really didn't want her staying with me. I wanted

145

Brett to stay with me, that was what I wanted, and the two things seemed mutually exclusive. Having heard her moaning on my sofa last night, I had no intention of having her there tonight listening to me. Then an idea popped into my head. 'Kimberly, do you have your bag with you with all your things in it?

'Yes. Big Ben dropped me off with it this morning. I could stay with him quite happily. I'm sure he didn't mean that he never sleeps with the same woman twice.'

I was sure he did mean it. My idea was better than sending her to stay with Big Ben though. 'Kimberly I will have Jane from the office come to collect you. Stay at work. She will not be long.'

We disconnected, and I called Jane. She was at home with her boyfriend but said she could collect Kimberly. I told her where to take her and confirmed she could get all that done and then be back at my place for her date with Bartholomew in time.'

Twenty minutes had ticked by while I was on the phone, but it was still not my turn to be dealt with at the equipment and uniform store. I wondered if the old lady that worked there had been instructed by CI Quinn to make me wait.

I kept checking my watch as the time ticked by. I needed to get away and meet up with Jane and Big Ben at my apartment. I wasn't sure if Patience would even turn up. I had sent her a text but got no reply. I could only imagine what Quinn had said to her or punished her with.

Finally, all my gear was handed over and, with a final signature, I was done.

It was gone seven when I escaped the police station, the shift had changed over while I was downstairs handing over my uniform, but even though the people I had to walk by hadn't been present to see my shame earlier, they would all know about it. Rumour was rife in the police station, much as it was in any closed environment. A couple of them tried to talk to me, but I shook my head that I was in no mood and left them behind.

It was so late that any rush hour traffic was long gone so the journey home was swift. My favourite spot in front of my building was empty. As I parked in it, I saw that the car to the left of mine was Jane's. She was sitting in it checking her reflection in the fold-down mirror. She had a date tonight and we were already behind schedule.

She saw me, folded the mirror up and got out of her car as I climbed out of mine. Across from us, another car door shut, and we both turned to see Big Ben. I had never seen Big Ben's car before. Maybe he had more than one, he certainly appeared to have some money. Not like Brett had money, but enough that he saw no need to work. Anyway, he was walking away from a huge black Ford Ranger. It had black paint and black wheels and a whole load of body kit bolted on to make it look meatier than the standard model would. Across the fold-down tailgate, I read the word Deranged.

It fitted.

'I was starting to wonder where you were. Everything okay?' he asked, crossing the carpark to join us.

'I have had better days.' I turned to face Jane. 'Kimberly settled in?'

'Yes, no problem. I think she will be very comfortable.'

'Where is she?' Big Ben asked.

'I stashed her at Tempest's house. I don't think Bartholomew will find her there.'

He chuckled. 'Did you tell Tempest?'

'Nope. He left me here with this mess, so he can have an unexpected house guest for a night or so. I doubt he will ever know it happened. I will clean the bed sheets and remake his bed before he returns.'

We had gone into the building and were standing in front of my door as I fiddled with my keys. The door across the landing opened.

'Amanda?' Mrs Fox called from her doorway.

'Hi, Mrs Fox.'

'There was a flower delivery for you earlier, dear. I let the man in and put them on your kitchen counter.'

'Thank you, Mrs Fox.' She was a sweet old lady. No doubt Brett had sent them in advance of our date tonight with a little message attached.

I pushed the door open, bent to scoop some mail from the carpet and walked through to the main room while shuffling it to see if it was anything other than bills.

'Wow!' came Jane's voice from behind me. I looked up to see an enormous spray of flowers sitting on my kitchen counter. The stems disappeared into one of those water bubbles things trapped inside a box. The box though had a compartment at the bottom, a flap that was hanging open.

I moved to look inside but caught something moving out of the corner of my eye. Over by my fruit bowl. Hadn't I seen something?

'Guys make yourself comfy. I'll put the kettle on,' I called over my shoulder as I lifted a banana.

A tarantula ran up my arm.

I froze for a second, completely unable to move as my brain tried to process the horror I felt. Then it got to my elbow and kept coming, which was altogether too much spider getting far too close to my face.

I screamed and flicked my arm to rid myself of the hairy, black menace. It shot across the room and flew in front of Jane's face.

'Aaaaaaargh!' said Jane. She got up and ran for the door as I spotted another tarantula emerging from behind my bin, its front two legs extended in the air like a threat.

'Amanda, you have a spider problem,' Big Ben advised me as he started towards the door as well, he was pointing to another three huge, hairy spiders that were climbing my curtains.

I ran, my heart threatening to burst from my chest and I didn't stop until I had gone down all the stairs and was out in the street. Big Ben sauntered out a few seconds after me, far too cool to run or show that he was scared.

He already had a phone to his ear and was informing the police about my latest predicament.

'Thank you. I believe we will wait outside.' He hung up. 'The police will be here soon along with animal control. You may want to consider sleeping somewhere else tonight.'

Miserable, I slumped onto the bonnet of my car. How was Bartholomew doing this? How had he even had time? Although perhaps he already had the spiders, and it had been hours since he was released from the station. It was enough time to buy flowers and drop them off.

'I need a drink.'

'Jane,' Big Ben called. Jane was sitting in her car looking quite freaked out. 'Jane dear, why don't you two ladies go across the road and get a drink? I'll call you when the police arrive.' He produced a crisp twenty-pound note from somewhere and stuffed it into my hand. 'Go,' he insisted, his voice gentle.

Then my feet were moving. Jane had hold of my hand and was pulling me across the street to the pub there. I don't remember much about it. Mostly Jane kept hold of my left hand and pushed a glass of something dark and strong into my right. It turned out to be brandy. My brain was on lockdown. It had taken a break from operating my body. There were spiders in my apartment. This morning there had been a giant snake in my car and now I had a dozen tarantulas in my home. I was freaking out.

Presently, the brandy was gone, and Big Ben came into the pub to find us. We were tucked into a corner by ourselves. A couple of young lads had spotted the two girls sitting unattended a while ago and had sauntered over full of swagger. I hadn't even looked up, but I did hear Jane tell them to go away in her deep voice. I might have laughed had my brain been working.

'There is a team in your apartment now trying to catch all the spiders,' Big Ben told me. 'It might take them a while because they don't know how many there are and don't want to leave any behind.' I didn't want that either. 'The police came and took a statement from your neighbour across the hall. I'm not sure she was much help, she just kept saying it was a young black man that delivered the flowers.'

'They will want a statement from me,' I whispered, my voice barely loud enough for me to hear. I was trying to get myself moving. I hated spiders. It had run up my arm and I wondered if I would ever feel clean again.

'Shall we get this done?' Big Ben asked, pulling gently on my hand to get me back on my feet. 'You can crash at my place until they give you the all clear.' He was being very sweet, it was a caring, compassionate side of Big Ben that I had never seen before.

He held my hand to keep me steady, perhaps seeing how unsteady I was on my feet, and guided me over to where there were two police cars.

Sgt Dave Barnet took a statement from me and let me go. Someone handed me my bag. It had been left on the kitchen counter next to the flowers where I had put it down.

There was a squeeze to my arm. I turned to see Jane next to me. 'I'm going home, Amanda. Don't worry about tonight, I have already messaged Bartholomew and apologised for cancelling at the last moment. He said he was fine with rearranging the date for another night. We can work things out in the morning.' She had missed the date with Bartholomew. We were going to lead him into a trap. None of it had happened. Jane gave me a little hug and was gone.

I heard Big Ben confirm that Sgt Barnet had no further need for me to remain at the scene. They would call to confirm when the animal control chaps were done. He still had hold of my hand, so he led me to his car, put me on the passenger's seat and took me to his flat.

Halfway there, Big Ben started talking. 'Hotstuff. I have been trying to work out if I have ever had a woman in my flat that I haven't had sex with. You don't have to be the first, you know.'

'Oh my God, Ben. Seriously, you're trying to get in my knickers now?'

'It seems like the best thing for you. You have had a nasty shock, so let's take your mind off it. I assure you I'm very good.'

We had arrived at his building. 'Benjamin, I honestly have no idea how you ever get a woman into your bed. If I had a better option, I would be going there now and not planning to sleep on your sofa.'

'Yeah, you're planning to sleep on my sofa. Good luck resisting me once you enter … the lair.' He put extra emphasis on the last two words and dropped his voice to make it sound sinister. I rolled my eyes and told myself he was just messing around. I sure hoped he was.

Big Ben came around the car to open my door. I climbed out but stood up too quickly and went a little dizzy. He caught me as I all but fell out of his giant four by four car.

'Are you okay?'

'I think so. Just a head spin.' I stood up straight, but he kept his arm around me for support as he led me to the building. A tender, helpful version of Big Ben was something of a revelation.

His building was much nicer than mine. That it was housed inside a gated community that had a security guard checking the people coming in said a lot. It also meant that money invested in the beautiful grounds around the buildings did not get ruined by wandering teens, homeless people or anyone else. The lobby of his building had a marble floor, and the stairs were chrome and glass and utterly spotless. He pressed the button to call the lift.

Halfway up to his penthouse suite, I suddenly felt my heart drop. In all the horror and excitement, I had forgotten my date with Brett. I yanked my phone from my bag and dialled his number. No signal.

Impatient for five seconds that felt like five minutes, the lift arrived at its destination with me shoving the doors open to get out while simultaneously hitting the redial button. The clock on the phone told me it was quarter after eight. Brett must be outside my apartment.

It rang for a while before it connected. Then Brett's voice came on the phone, but it wasn't the usual sexy tone that I always got. Instead, he sounded bored. Monosyllabic.

'Brett, God I'm so sorry. There were some flowers delivered to my house, and I thought they were from you, but they weren't of course. They were from …'

'I saw you with him, Amanda.'

'You ... sorry, what? You saw me with who?'

'The tall guy. I saw you drive away in his car, then I saw you hugging him before you went arm in arm into a building.'

'Oh, Brett. You have it all wrong.' He'd seen me with Big Ben. Now he was feeling betrayed, as I might if the roles were switched, but it was all a mistake.

'Amanda, I don't own you. We haven't slept together. I just didn't expect there to be someone else.'

'No, Brett, please listen,' I begged. I just needed him to hear what I was saying but he didn't want to hear me.

'Don't call me, Amanda. Okay?' he didn't wait for me to answer though. He just hung up.

I stared at the wall defeated. I was having such an awful day. Bartholomew and CI Quinn, Patience wasn't talking to me, my home was full of spiders. I was getting nowhere with my case and now Brett thought I was cheating on him. I refused to cry. A defiant tear rolled down my cheek anyway and for the second time today I started sobbing.

I was so fed up being at the bottom. Being on the losing end. Big Ben placed his hands on my shoulders and steered me inside his apartment, wheeled me in front of his couch and handed me a mug of tea as I sat.

I mumbled my thanks, gave myself a mental shake and sent Brett a text explaining what he'd seen. I wanted to call him, to have him come and get me and take me back to his place. I wanted to have sex with him and put this silly misunderstanding behind us.

It was a long text that took many drafts before I pressed send. My tea was cool by the time I was done. Cooler than I would have wanted it, but it was nice that Big Ben had made it for me. Sitting on the couch with my feet tucked beneath me and feeling a little pathetic and battered from my day, I pondered what I would do now.

The simplest thing was to spend the night on Big Ben's couch and go home in the morning. I expected it would be clear of giant, killer spiders by then. I would need to thoroughly clean the whole apartment, which wouldn't be a simple task as I would be holding a large mallet in one hand just in case animal control had missed one.

Big Ben sauntered back into the central living area. He had nothing on his top half, revealing, not for the first time, his lean, muscular torso. He looked like he could run through walls. In his arms, he was carrying bedding and pillows to make up the couch for me.

'How are you doing now?' he asked.

'Much better, thank you,' I lied.

'It sounded like man trouble earlier. Do you want to talk about it?'

'Not really.'

'Fair enough. I didn't know you were involved with anyone. Is it serious?' he asked.

I couldn't decide if Big Ben was being nosy or just making conversation. I gave him the benefit of the doubt, 'I had hoped it was going to be serious, but we never got quite that far. We had a date tonight and it… well, tonight happened, didn't it? Anyway, he saw me with you and jumped to a conclusion.'

Big Ben nodded. 'I always figured you would end up with Tempest. That's why I have never turned on the charm around you. He's my bro and it was obvious that he was interested.'

'Never turned on the charm? Benjamin, you talk as if all you need do is smile and girls fall into your bed.'

'Err, yup. That is pretty much how it works. Shall I demonstrate?'

I rolled my eyes. 'You really think this is going to happen?'

'Actually, no.'

'Good.'

'Not tonight. Maybe later this week. You're all fired up with resistance right now.'

'Ben, it's not going to happen.'

He stared at me with curiosity on his face. 'Amanda, you are truly a strange lady. So, I'm going to leave you to get some sleep. If you change your mind in the night, you know where to find me. Off you go.'

'Off I ... Huh? Where am I going?' Now I was bewildered.

'I'm on the couch, Amanda. One does not invite a guest to one's house and then have them sleep on the furniture. You're in my bed. I just put all fresh linen on it for you. There is a door to take you through to the bathroom if you want a shower. There is a range of ladies' toiletries and cosmetics in the cupboard beneath the sink.'

Of course, he had ladies' toiletries waiting.

He made little, go-away motions with his hand until I got up and went in the direction he was pointing. His bedroom was a sumptuous thing, decorated in stark black and white with splashes of blood red here and there. The bed itself was a huge white cast iron frame with mirrors on three walls around it and, when I looked up, more mirrors on the ceiling. I pushed the door closed behind me. I would attend to my ablutions in a minute. I felt suddenly tired, and the bed looked very comfortable. I would just lay down for a little bit.

Sleeping with Friends

WEDNESDAY, NOVEMBER 2ND 0722HRS

An odd sensation pulled me from my slumber. Only my eyes were moving, but all wasn't as I had left it. Big Ben was in the bed with me and his heavy arm was draped across my midriff. I had fallen asleep on the bed without even so much as cleaning my teeth. I felt scuzzy now and my bladder was full, so I needed to move.

His arm was on top of the covers, pinning them to me. I was still dressed thankfully, though I wondered if he would be also. Carefully, I slid out from beneath his arm and stepped silently into the bathroom. Once I had the door closed, I realised that I did not know where the light switch was and had to fumble to find it.

I would clean myself up, let myself out and walk back across town to my own place like I was doing the walk of shame. I would call Big Ben later and thank him for his hospitality and never mention that he'd joined me in bed.

When I came out of the bathroom though he was awake. The light in the bedroom was on and he was missing. The clock claimed it to be just after half past seven. I grabbed my phone to see if I had messages from Brett. I did not. Nor did I have anything from Patience, which was highly unusual and could only be attributed to my landing her in hot water yesterday. I would have to go to her apartment later if I was unable to raise a response by any other method.

There was noise coming from the living area. Big Ben had the TV on and in the kitchen the smell of coffee brewing was beginning to filter through.

'Good morning,' I called out as I went in. Big Ben appeared from the kitchen. He was dressed in sports gear thankfully. I had been mildly concerned he might not bother with clothes in his own environment. In his hands, he had two mugs of coffee on a tray with a pot of sugar and a small milk jug in the shape of a cow. He was far more domesticated than he gave rise to believe.

'Good morning, Amanda. I hope I didn't disturb your sleep last night. I found that I'm too long to be comfortable on the sofa, so I slid in next to you.'

'That's okay,' I said, not entirely sure that it was. I wanted to go home, but it would be rude to rush out now when he'd made me coffee and was being surprisingly sweet and supportive.

'You look constantly surprised when I do something selfless for you?' He said, picking up my reaction as he sat on one of a pair of leather sofas. 'I believe you may have the wrong opinion of me.'

'Benjamin, by your own admission you plan to have sex with every eligible woman you can. Never caring about them, always moving on. Do you not think that a psychologist would say that you're trying to fill a void in your life? Have you ever thought about what that might be?'

'Babe, I filled several voids last weekend,' he quipped back.

I made a vomiting motion in reply. 'Do you have to be so crude all the time?'

'I'm just giving you a fighting chance. You seem determined that you don't wish to sleep with me. I don't understand it, but I figure if I make you feel uncomfortable it will prolong the inevitable day when you throw yourself at me.'

'So, you're acting like a cocky git for my sake?'

'Is it working? Do you feel like parting your legs for me right now?'

'Eww, no.'

'There you go then.' He fell silent.

I slugged down my coffee. 'I really think I ought to be going?' I announced getting up.

'Wow. I was only not being a cocky git for a few seconds and already the effect is wearing off. You better run before my natural magnetism takes hold.' He was laughing as I threw a cushion at him and went out of his door.

Investigating a Ghost on a Ghost Tour

With a renewed sense of purpose, I set about my day. My apartment was in need of a severe tidying. It hadn't been trashed, but the team that had come in to take the tarantulas out had moved things about. My furniture was out of place, my curtains ruffled in an unsettling way that suggested there might still be a giant spider hiding behind them and I knew of course that there had been a dozen strangers in my house last night, all leaving their fingerprints behind, all touching my belongings, riffling through my drawers. I shuddered at the thought. I was left with a sense of violation.

The apartment would have to wait though. I was going to do something positive with my day. I was going to solve the Tonbridge Wells ghost tour case, I was going to make peace with Patience, and I was going to get my boyfriend back. First, I needed a shower, some breakfast and a change of clothes.

Thirty minutes later I was going out of my door. I was clean, dressed and had a belly full of toast and eggs. I was heading to Tempest's house. I had intended to check in on Kimberly but had forgotten to do so and she would be on her way to work by now. I could call her but if she wanted anything, she would have called me already. I sent a text to Patience that I hoped she would pick up and answer. A text from Brad last night had confirmed that she had been suspended without pay. I was offering to help with that by giving her paid work with the firm. I wasn't entirely sure I could do that, but Tempest had left me in charge, so I was making my own rules.

Jane's car was on Tempest's driveway as it had been before, and she was inside at the computer. The first thing I noticed was that the computer now had three screens.

'Hi, Jane. Been making some upgrades?'

'Hi, Amanda,' she replied, not turning away from what she was doing. 'Having one screen was slowing me down. I'm running too many different applications simultaneously. I brought these from home.'

'Is that Meet Market?' I asked seeing the right-hand screen.

'Yeah. I have been rearranging my date with Bartholomew. I didn't know if that was still something we wanted to do, but I figured I could easily cancel it if I needed to.'

'Did he bite?'

'He did. While we were in the pub and you were a little…'

'Catatonic.' I filled in the blank she had left.

'I sent him a message saying I had to cancel but wanted to rearrange. He was fine with it, better than I expected, but I said I needed to work out when I would next be free. All I need to do now is tell him when.'

'How about tonight?'

I watched as she typed the same words into the message box and sent it away. Then she turned to face me. 'If you go after Bartholomew now, will it not open you up to a harassment case?'

'It could. However, I know he's guilty. Kimberly is sleeping in the boss's house, and Bartholomew's targeting me with spiders and snakes with no sign of stopping until I stop him. I don't feel much choice other than to catch him out and prove that I was right from the start.'

'How about the Tonbridge Wells ghost tour's ghost?' Jane asked. 'They sent several gigabytes of data yesterday that made the computer go a bit wobbly when I opened it. Thankfully they sent it via a transfer service, so it didn't flood the cache memory.

Jane was babbling computer nerd speak again. I had no idea what she was telling me, other than we now had footage of the moments when Sir Chelios visited.

'Did they send a list of names?' I asked.

'That was the only other file they sent. I printed it.' Jane handed me a sheet of A4 paper. There were thirteen names on it, almost all women, only two men and they had the same last name as two of the women.

'I'm going to call them. Can you see if any of them are linked please?' I left Jane to it and took a seat at the dining table Tempest had shoved up against one wall. I started at the top of the list but got no answer. The second name, a lady by the name Agatha Milford did answer.

I got a breezy, 'Good morning.' With a voice that screamed Royal Tonbridge Wells with extra emphasis on the Royal bit.

'Good morning, Mrs Milford. My name is Amanda Harper. I'm a detective with the Blue Moon Investigation Agency and have been contracted by Lily Hallett at

Tonbridge Ghost Tours to investigate some odd occurrences they have experienced. Do you have a few minutes to talk to me please?'

'Yes, of course. Lily said you might call.' That struck me as odd. If I was a customer of a tour I would most likely be a tourist. Let's suggest that I have that wrong though and Agatha is a local, she certainly sounded like one. However, what is the likelihood that I would know the tour operator by her first name? It could just be a coincidence, and the two ladies did indeed know each other. I continued.

'Mrs Milford can you explain to me what you experienced when you took the ghost tour, please? Give as much detail as you can.'

As requested, she launched into a lengthy account of the night she took the tour. About a minute into her story, I started to feel that it was rehearsed. At no point did she um or ah or pause. Perhaps she was just very articulate, but her story was so well polished that it felt like I was being read a script. She finished with, 'Then a chill of absolute dread fell upon me as I felt his presence drift through my soul. He whispered his name and was gone.' Agatha lapsed into silence.

'Is there anything else?' I enquired.

'No, no. I think that is about all I remember.' She had remembered everything. I thanked her for her time, made a couple of notes and called the next number. The lady that answered this time was Susan Haverhill. Once again, I explained who I was and what I wanted. Once again, she agreed to tell me what she knew, but if she was as familiar with Lily Hallett as Agatha was, she gave no sign.

I let her tell me about her experience at the ghost tour. She rambled more than Agatha had but she used many of the same words to describe what she had seen, so much so that it began to sound like the same story, just told differently. I was smelling something very fishy about the whole case but knew I had been duped when Susan said, 'A chill of dread passed through me as I felt his presence touch my soul.' It was almost verbatim what Agatha had said.

'Do you know Agatha Milford?' I asked. Susan spluttered a little when claiming that she did not. I was certain she was lying. Not only at that point, but since she started speaking.

I thanked her for her time and disconnected. Turning to Jane, I found her waiting patiently for me to get off the phone.

'They all know the client,' she said, which concluded the case. Less than thirty minutes of actual investigation and we had solved the case.

'I was just about to ask what you had found out because it's clearly all fake.' Jane indicated to the screens with her head. 'Show me.'

I crossed the room and leaned to see what Jane had found. Social media provided a link between every name on the list and Lily Hallett. I dismissed the notion that it could be a coincidence. That Lily Hallett had been so keen to have Tempest at her office and wanted to take photographs had tipped her hand. This was all about publicity.

I thought about that for a moment. Lily Hallett had invented a ghost that was visiting her tour, probably one she had researched and for which a legend already existed. Tempest had been involved in a couple of high-profile cases recently, so while he was hardly a household name, in the local community, especially those involved in any form of business that had a connection to the paranormal, he was known. Did a visit by him then legitimise her tour? Give it greater credibility and interest?

Probably.

I was ready to believe that this had been her intention, but what did I do about it? She had contracted the agency to investigate her case. Did I string it out and charge her a fat fee for my trouble? Did I reveal the scam to her, but have Tempest agree to a few photographs since she was paying? I didn't like the second option. It felt cheesy. Tempest is very clear that the paranormal isn't real, so I couldn't see him endorsing a ghost tour.

I decided to give myself some time to consider it. I had still not heard from Patience, so I was going to drive to her flat and knock on her door. I needed to make things right between us.

Jane and I made a plan to meet at my place at seven o'clock again to make ready for the date and I left her practicing speaking with a girl's voice. She was rubbish at it.

Where is Patience?

I tried calling on my way over, just in case my persistence paid off. There was no reply though. I also called Brett. I had been putting it off because in my desperation to resolve our hiccup I was worried he wouldn't listen and continue to reject me. I hated the idea that we would break up after our first little fight, especially since it was all a mistake.

His phone rang at the other end though and just when I thought it was going to switch to an answering service, a woman answered instead.

It was his assistant, Janice. 'Hi, Amanda,' she chirped happily. Janice seemed to know everything about him, so if he changed his status to available or single it hadn't made it to her ears yet. 'Are you after Brett? Duh, of course, you are. Why would I ask that when you were calling his phone?' I hadn't met Janice yet. She had answered his phone a couple of times and had called me to arrange his social diary once when he was in a meeting and needed to delay a date. My mental image of her was a nineteen-year-old ditzy blonde, stereotypically pretty but not all that bright. Her brain seemed to flit from one idea to the next, never stopping in one place for very long.

'Hi, Janice. Is he there?'

'No, he flew to Bahrain this morning.'

'Did he have a meeting?'

'Not one that was on his calendar.'

'Do you know how long he is going to be away?'

'He said two or three days, but he didn't say what he was going there for, other than he needed a break. Are you guys okay? He seemed different this morning like he was upset about something. Ooh, did you guys have a fight?'

I distracted her with a question, 'Janice does he have a different phone with him?'

'Yes,' she said very carefully. 'I'm not allowed to give the number out to anyone though.'

'I'm his girlfriend, Janice. He would want me to have it.'

Janice gave it up after a minute or so cajoling. I thanked her and dialled the new number.

It was answered immediately. 'Brett Barker.'

My heart skipped. 'Brett. It's Amanda.'

'That Janice. I swear I need to fire her.' I tried to speak but he cut me off. 'Look, Amanda. I know you're going to protest your innocence, but I saw what I saw. I'm going away for a couple of days, kitesurfing with some friends. When I get back, if I want to call you to talk about it, I will. That's the best I can offer right now.'

'Okay, Brett,' I conceded with a tear on my cheek.

'I was really into you, Amanda.' He paused, and I waited while he framed what he wanted to say next. 'Now I just don't know. Don't call me, okay. I'll call you.'

He disconnected, leaving me feeling very lonely in my little car. Tempest was away, Patience was upset with me, more than she ever had been in all the years I had known her, Brett and I were on a break at the very best and my mum and her boyfriend were in Miami or wherever their cruise ship was currently. I needed more friends.

I had arrived at Patience's place. I was starting to feel angry about having to chase her. It wasn't my fault that Quinn is such a dick. I had suffered worse than her, she was getting some extra time off and I was offering her better-paying work to fill her spare time. I couldn't keep it up though. However bad I felt for myself, I knew that her current predicament was my fault. I trudged up the stairs to ring her doorbell.

There was no answer though. No sound of movement even from inside the apartment. Had she seen me coming and hidden? Was she so upset with me that she was avoiding me now? I knew she was here because her car was outside. I guess the pervy mechanic had finally finished with it and she had retrieved it yesterday after getting suspended.

I hammered on the door. 'Come on, Patience. Please open the door so we can talk!' I yelled so she would hear me. Still no sound from inside. I thumped hard on the door again.

'Shhhhh!' Came an insistent voice as a door opened across the other side of the landing. 'Keep it down, won't you? My husband works nights.'

Embarrassed, I turned to see a small woman in her late thirties in house slippers and flannel pyjamas with a towelling dressing gown hanging open to show her flabby middle. The overhang of her belly was visibly hanging lower than her top could cover.

'Sorry,' I apologised. 'Have you seen Patience?'

'Here, I have a key,' she said, producing a small keyring with a fluffy cupcake on it from inside her house. She shuffled across the landing, her slippers making a scuffing noise as they hung off the back of her feet to lightly scrape the tile.

She opened the door for me and stood back. 'I don't think she is there,' she told me as she popped a cigarette in her mouth. 'Haven't heard a thing all night or this morning so she is probably on a shift, love.'

I went inside as she inhaled deeply on the foul stick of putrid death. I would have to come back out through it soon enough. She was right in that Patience wasn't at home. I also knew that she wasn't at work unless I had been misinformed about her suspension, which seemed unlikely. Unless CI Quinn had found her an even more unpleasant task and called her back in.

I went to her bedroom, opened her wardrobe and counted her uniforms hanging there. Only three, so one was missing. To be sure, I went to her bathroom and opened the laundry basket. The missing uniform was there, discarded for washing after she came home yesterday. So, I knew she had come home yesterday but not where she was now.

I wrote her a text to tell her I was in her apartment and was worried about her and was wondering where she was. I pressed send, then heard her phone chirp.

It was in the house.

'Patience?' I called out, wondering if she was hiding in a cupboard. No sound came back, so I called her phone and when it connected and started ringing a second later, I found it abandoned on the kitchen counter, hidden from view behind a box of Weetoes.

This wasn't good.

'Are you going to be long?' her neighbour asked, leaning into the doorway at the front of the apartment so I could see her.

Patience's apartment showed no sign that she had been

taken by force. Everything was in place, but like most people she never went anywhere without her phone and if she went anywhere, she took her car. I told myself I had no reason to panic. Not yet. But a sense of dread was claiming first prize in the race for the pit of my stomach anyway.

I waved to her neighbour that I was coming, took Patience's phone and went out the door expressing my thanks for her help, while simultaneously holding my breath to avoid the foul smoke.

It was almost noon when I called the station to see if anyone had heard from Patience or knew where she was. It was Sgt Dave Barnet that answered the phone.

'Hi, Amanda. What can I do for you?' He asked after I spoke.

'Have you, or anyone else, seen or heard from Patience? She is missing.'

'Missing? In what way?'

'Her car is outside her place, her phone was inside her flat, but she is not there, and her neighbour claims she didn't hear her last night.'

'She did seem quite upset when she left here yesterday. Are you sure she is not just avoiding you while she calms down?' he asked.

'She might have been, but I don't think that is what she is doing now. Why would she leave her phone behind?'

'Have you been calling her?'

'Well, yes.'

'Then perhaps she wanted some distance.'

'What about her car?'

'Does she have sisters? Other friends? Parents with a car? Anyone of them could have picked her up.'

He was being completely logical, which was really unhelpful because I wanted to jump to conclusions. I would get nowhere with this though, so I thanked him for his help and disconnected.

Sitting in my car, I pulled out Patience's phone and scrolled to find her sisters and her mum. I dialled each of them, but they did not know where she was either.

Her older sister Charity had some thoughts on the matter though, 'Girlfriend, that 'ho is probably in bed with some random man. She always did like the dick. She's that much of a slut, if she went to buy candy, she would end up getting pick 'n' dicks.'

Wow.

No help from her family then. I still doubted she was with a man, but I couldn't think of anything I could do about her absence immediately. Reluctantly, I jabbed my ignition switch and set off for Royal Tonbridge Wells where I proposed to confront Lily Hallett.

Ghost Tours My Backside

It took over an hour to get to Lily Hallett's office because I stopped for some lunch on the way. I found a global coffee chain outlet not far from her office where I bought a giant cup of mochaccino and a sandwich. The range of cakes were calling my name from the display counter. Somehow, I resisted, despite feeling that I deserved a treat to counterbalance the awfulness of the last couple of days.

Refuelled, I left the car where it was in a multi-story car park and walked around the corner to the Ghost Tours office. Through the glass front of her office, I could see Lily talking to a small group of what appeared to be Chinese tourists. I went inside and waited patiently.

There were leaflets to look at and some posters on the wall advertising the tour and what one could expect. It was in several languages. Thankfully, Lily concluded her business with the tourists before I ran out of things to inspect. She saw them to the door then turned to face me, a smile on her face and her hand outstretched for shaking.

'Hello again, Miss Hallett.'

'Do you have news about when Tempest will be able to visit?' she asked.

'That is what I came to see you about, actually. Shall we sit?'

Lily's face betrayed her excitement at the possibility of having Tempest visit. I hadn't yet found the time to call him. I could have, of course, but I was still a little angry about his sudden absence and I didn't want to find myself berating him as I unloaded all my problems from this week.

I sat in the same chair I had two days ago when we reached her office in the back corner. 'So, Amanda, when will I get to meet the great Tempest Michaels.'

'That will be down to him I'm afraid, Miss Hallett. I haven't talked to him about it yet.'

'I don't understand,' she replied, looking confused. 'You said you were here to discuss his visit.'

'No, I said I was here to see you about your desire to have him visit. Tempest does not believe in the paranormal, supernatural world and most certainly does not believe in ghosts. He is a good investigator though. So, how long do you think it would have taken him to discover that all of the people that claimed to have been touched by or to have heard Sir Chelios were your friends?'

Her face coloured and she opened her mouth to answer me. No words came out though as she tried a couple of times to frame the next lie.

'You gave me their names and phone numbers. It was obvious they were reading from a script or had been coached in what to say.'

'Well, I… ah.'

'Look. You hired the Agency for an investigation. The case

is now closed, and I have a bill for you. There are no hard feelings and you're not the first one to have made it all up. This was just a publicity stunt though, wasn't it? You wanted pictures of Tempest at your premises so you could legitimise your ghost tour and have something interesting to Tweet about, yes?'

'Yes,' she said with some grumpy resignation. She had been staring down at her lap but looked up now to lock eyes with me. 'Was it really that easy to work out?'

'It took the office assistant less than thirty minutes to connect all the witnesses.'

'The office assistant,' she echoed. 'Do you think Tempest will pose for a photo with me?' she wasn't willing to let the idea go. Maybe she was right, and this would generate business for her.

'I can't say,' I replied. 'You could just ask him yourself though. Had you done that you could have avoided all the subterfuge and the bill.

'How much is the bill, please?' she asked as if she hadn't thought about it until now.

'I will have Jane at the office finalise your account and invoice you tomorrow. It will be in line with the fees I described during our first meeting, but more than it would have been if you had just asked him. Oh, and I want all the photographs you took of me, please. I do not give you permission to use my image for your publicity.' It had suddenly occurred to me that she might.

Lily promised me that she wouldn't use the pictures and would send anything that had been printed off to the business address. It wouldn't stop the photographer from making copies, there was nothing I could do about that, but Lily understood the repercussions of using my image without permission, so I doubted she would.

She walked me to the door, apologised for her misguided actions and seemed quite glad that I was going.

Meandering back to the car park I checked my watch to find that our little chat had lasted almost an hour. It was just before three o'clock, so I would have to get a move on, or I would get caught in the school run traffic again.

Interesting News

On the way home, I had gone via Patience's house again. I had her phone so if she had resurfaced, she wouldn't be able to call me, and I couldn't call her. Her car was still there and just as before I got no answer from her door. I knocked on her neighbour's door but got no answer there either.

I hung around for a while trying to decide what I should do. Patience could be anywhere. She could be shacked up with a man that I didn't know about, she could have taken a taxi to the station and headed into London for the day for some stress-releasing retail therapy and she simply forgot to pick her phone up. Or she could have been grabbed by Bartholomew and his entourage and be getting tortured to death right now.

I knew I wouldn't be able to convince the guys at the station to do anything official about her. She wouldn't be officially considered a missing person until the third day and even when her absence was acknowledged, it's hard to find a missing person. You had to get lucky and find someone who had seen them being taken, if that was what had happened or had seen them going somewhere and you kept going, following the breadcrumb trail until you found them. Except... all too often what we found was the missing person's body.

I didn't know what to do. What would Tempest do? I asked myself. He would get hold of everyone he could and rally them to help him.

The answer wasn't much help as I was struggling to come up with people to call. Big Ben would be ready to help, but I worried that would be just because he wanted another shot at getting into my knickers.

I would need him tonight anyway. Jane had rearranged her date with Bartholomew. Same place and same time as last night. I prayed there would be no surprise waiting for me in my apartment this time to scupper the plan. I was convinced that Bartholomew was dangerous, that he was capable of hurting people. I had no proof though.

Thinking about proof, I remembered Kimberly's toiletries in the lab at the station. I needed to get them back, so I could have them tested. What would that cost? Who would I even approach to do it? Tempest had said something once about a chemistry teacher at a school or a college he knew. If he'd told me the fellow's name or which school, I couldn't now remember.

On my way back to my place from Patience's, I called the lab's number hoping that Simon or Steve would pick up. I owed them an apology as well.

'Crime lab,' Simon said as he picked up the phone.

'Simon, it's Amanda.'

'Oh, hey, Amanda. Are you calling about all the toiletries we still have?'

'Yes, can I come and get them? I still want to have them

tested.' Maybe Simon could tell me where I could take them.

'CI Quinn ordered us to throw it all out,' Simon told me flatly.

The news felt like a gut punch.

'We ignored him, of course. Hold on I'm putting you on speakerphone.' I

listened as the phone clicked a couple of times, then the tone of noise changed to provide the echoing effect one gets from an enclosed room on a speaker.

'Hi, Amanda.' It was Steve's voice.

'Hi, Steve.'

'I analysed the shampoo bottle. It was all we had time for so far. The rest of it we hid in case he came back. The first piece of news is that you were right.'

I fist bumped the air.

'Someone tampered with the lady's shampoo, and they knew what they were doing. Do you need to write this down, because it's about to get scientific? Never mind, I'll send you a report.'

I really didn't need the long-winded version, but I knew they both liked to show off how clever they were and had learned to indulge them long ago. It meant they would do things for me that they wouldn't for others. Like right now for instance.

I was crawling through traffic anyway, so it might take a while to get home and now I had company in the car, sort of. Steve started his explanation. 'When making a hair removal product you need a chemical that will attack the keratin faster than the skin can produce a new supply of keratin. This is not easy because in doses high enough to do this most chemicals will be dangerous to the person using them. One also must avoid unpleasant odours which such a chemical might bring and there are side effects like eczema associated with any strong hair removal product. What has been used, is an exquisite blend that is attacking the sulphur bonds in the keratin through a salt of thioglycolic acid. However, for that to work, it has to exist as an active dianion in the product.'

I honestly understood only about twenty-five percent of the words he was saying. It reminded me of taking German classes in school, where I knew some words so would listen to Herr Schneider prattle on and be able to pick out odd words here and there that I knew. The flow of what he was saying would be lost to me though. This was the same.

'This requires a high concentration of hydroxide ions,' he continued and then launched into a series of chemical formulas. I could feel my eyes getting heavy. If I had been on my sofa at home, I would be asleep already.

He finally wrapped up the lesson by saying, 'That's not even the interesting bit.'

'Wait, what? There is a complex chemical chain present in my client's shampoo that is causing her hair to fall out, it can only have been introduced deliberately and by someone with a very high level of chemical knowledge and that's not the interesting bit?'

'No, Amanda. The interesting bit is that we found anhydrous ammonia and iodine crystals in trace quantities on the outside of the bottle. These would have washed off if they had been exposed to running water in her shower. That is where you said you found the bottle, yes?'

'It is.' I had no idea where he was going with this new information.

'So, it can only have been introduced by the person you saw in her apartment,' he announced triumphantly. He was waiting for me to respond, and I was trying to think of something to say that wouldn't make me sound stupid.

'Um,' I tried.

'They are the base ingredients in making meth-amphetamine. You make that, then bubble acidic gas through it to make crystal meth. We have a massive crystal meth problem here. We have for years. Whoever it was that tampered with the shampoo, that same person had been making crystal meth.' I could hear the pride in his voice, he knew what this meant.

Bartholomew was the Magdalene King.

A horn blared. I had been lost in thought and was drifting out of my lane. 'Guys, where is the evidence now?'

'With us. We are going to stay late to test a few more of the products when the Chief has gone home.'

'Have you told anyone else about this?'

'No,' said Simon, speaking for the first time in several minutes. 'Who would we even tell? The chief will not listen.'

He was right. If Bartholomew was cooking crystal meth somewhere, I would need to have all the evidence before I acted, before I approached Quinn to coordinate a raid or even an investigation. Even with irrefutable evidence Quinn might still ignore me just to be annoying.

I thanked them both for being so great and promised them a big mention when I solved the case. Despite the slow traffic, I was almost home, and my thoughts were of Jane's date with Bartholomew tonight. I was going to be the spider that drew him into my web.

Preparing for Jane's Date

I had called Big Ben from the car just before I arrived home. He knocked on my door just a few minutes after I got in.

'Cup of tea?' I held up the kettle as he settled on my sofa.

'Yes, please. Hotstuff why is there a blanket on your sofa now?' he asked.

'Because it no longer feels clean, Benjamin,' I said pointedly.

'Because Kimberly and I rolled around naked on it,' he confirmed. 'Sorry about that. I'm fairly sure it's clean, but I can pay to have it professionally scrubbed if you wish. Or, you know. We could take a turn on it and maybe you would feel less bothered about it then.'

He hit me with a dangerously suggestive smile and made his pecs dance a bit beneath his shirt.

I rolled my eyes and flicked the kettle switch to on. I set out three cups expecting that Jane would be along soon enough.

'Thank you for doing this again, Benjamin.'

'You're welcome. Should we expect Patience shortly?'

'No, I don't think so. She has gone missing. Or rather, I don't know where she is.'

His face crinkled at the news. 'Missing? For how long?'

'Not long. Missing is the wrong word to use,' I said, wishing I could have said it differently. 'We had something of a falling out yesterday, at least I think we did. I got her into some trouble at work, and we haven't spoken since. I tried calling and sent her several text messages. So, today I went to her house, but she wasn't there. Her car was though and more worryingly, so was her phone.'

'Her phone?' he echoed.

I held it up to show him. I still had it.

There was a knock at my door. Jane had arrived. Big Ben got up to answer it as the kettle clicked off, the hot water inside reaching a rolling boil.

Jane came in looking spectacular. Her blonde wig swept over one shoulder, and her makeup was salon perfect. She appeared to be wearing a fake bra so that for the first time there were lumps in the front of her white silk top. I couldn't tell that it was a guy under the clothing. She had selected a long skirt that hugged her bum and ended mid-calf where thick tights took her legs the rest of the way to a pair of brand-new black heels. It might be a man's legs beneath the hosiery, but you would never know. As it was November, it was all complimented by a thick, long coat that fell to her knees in a superbly contrasting camel colour against the black of her skirt and the white of her top. It looked expensive. All in all, she was a knockout.

'Hi, Jane. I was just making tea.'

'Sounds great,' she replied. 'I feel like I could do with something stronger though. I'm quite nervous.'

'Do you want something?' I asked while doing a mental tally of what I might have in the house to offer her.

'No, that's okay. I had better not.' I noticed then that she was speaking in a passable falsetto version of the usual deep man's voice. I was used to the deep tone coming from the petite woman and no longer really noticed how incongruous it was. I guess she had been working on it.

'What's the plan tonight?' she asked, taking a seat on the sofa.

'You meet with Bartholomew as planned, have a couple of drinks, engage him in conversation and let's see what happens. I wouldn't let it drag out too long though. This is just a first date, if he has some ulterior motive guiding his actions then we want to know what it is, but I doubt you can straight out ask him.'

'Okay.'

'I should mention that the crime lab guys were able to prove that someone had tampered with Kimberly's shampoo. There was an exotic cocktail of carefully crafted chemicals in it that could only have been produced by a very knowledgeable chemist. There were also traces of chemicals on the outside of the shampoo bottle that suggest he is involved in the production of crystal meth.'

'Really? Big Ben and Jane said simultaneously.

'I think he is the Magdalene King. Someone the police have been after for more years than he has been alive, but I think maybe he has assumed the role or come into it by deposing the previous guy. I don't know, I'm still working out the idea, but I will be tailing him from now on.'

'Is there anything you specifically want me to ask him tonight? Or do I just make chit-chat and let him talk about whatever he wants?' Jane asked.

'You could maybe drop in about religion, see if he talks

about voodoo at all. Maybe ask what he does for a living, see if he brags about a shady side.'

Big Ben had a thought, 'You could say that bad boys are a bit of a turn on for you and see if he takes the bait. Lots of guys like to pretend to be the dangerous, gangster sort.'

'Time to go,' Jane said, checking the time on her phone and putting down her now empty teacup.

'We'll be back once it's done,' said Big Ben doing likewise.

'Hold on I'm coming with you.'

'Won't he recognise you?' Asked Jane.

'Give me one minute.' I rushed to the bedroom. I had been thinking about this for a few hours. I have some costume makeup from a Halloween event a few years back and outfits that will alter my appearance. If Jane could be a man dressed up to look like a completely convincing girl, then I could turn myself into a boy.

I had a short wig that I tucked all my hair into and a pair of men's cargo pants and paint-spattered caterpillar boots that had been left in my flat when I booted a cheating boyfriend out a couple of years back. His feet were only a size bigger than mine, so I used them when I had crappy tasks to do and didn't want to ruin anything of my own. I wiped off the little makeup I usually wore and used mascara to thicken the fine hairs on my face. It would be dark in the bar and all I needed to do was not look like Amanda Harper to Bartholomew. We would sit close enough to see him, but not so close that he would be able to notice me. I could probably sit with my back to him and let Big Ben do the surveillance bit anyway.

Satisfied that I looked manly enough to fool someone that wasn't looking at me, I went back out to find Big Ben and Jane standing by my door and waiting to go.

'Oh,' said Jane.

'Oh, good, or oh bad?' I asked.

'It'll do,' replied Big Ben. 'Although, you forgot one element in your transformation.'

I stepped to my right to look in the full-length mirror I had by the door. 'What?' I asked when I failed to see what to him was clearly obvious.

'Sweetie, you have rather large boobs.'

Oops. He was right.

'Too late now. Let's go.' With that, I pushed them both out of my apartment and down the stairs.

Jane's Date

When we arrived at the bar, Big Ben and I had gone in first. I spotted Bartholomew straight away, in a cubby not far from the bar. We took a table that was diagonally across the room from him and quite close to the door. I had a direct line of sight to watch him but sat so that my natural angle of vision wasn't on him. Big Ben went up the bar to order drinks and scope the rest of the bar just to see if Barty had any of his friends with him.

Big Ben wouldn't know what they looked like but was savvy enough to watch body language and spot two people looking at each other too often for it to be a coincidence.

A minute after we came in, timed so that we could have a quick look around and position ourselves, Jane came through the door.

Bartholomew had been watching and, through the wonders of modern internet dating, knew exactly what she looked like. I watched his face. He was very pleased to see her.

There wasn't much we could do now except hang on and see how Jane got on. Really, we were only there as a rescue squad if Jane wanted to bail.

Big Ben returned with two large gin cocktails and sat down adjacent to me. We could both watch the corner where Jane and Bartholomew were sitting, but both needed to avoid doing so in case we made it obvious.

'You were telling me about Patience,' Big Ben reminded me.

'Sorry, yes, Patience,' I said. 'Missing but officially, of course, she isn't.'

'How about unofficially?' His voice was guarded, or perhaps it was concern I was hearing, like if someone hurt her, he would make them pay.

'I don't know where she is and neither does anyone else. I spoke with her mum and her sisters, they mostly suggested she was to be found in bed with a man.'

'You don't think so though.' He said it as a statement.

'Patience always tells me about the men she meets. She told me more than I wanted to know about you. She hasn't mentioned anyone in the last week, so unless she met a guy last night, I don't think that is the answer.' Talking about it was making me more worried for her. Tomorrow I would need to press the chaps at the station to do something.

'Do you think he might have something to do with it?' he asked, meaning Bartholomew.

'I don't know.'

We both lapsed into silence and sipped our drinks. Neither of us wanted to have more than one drink tonight and had only chosen alcohol so we wouldn't stand out as the only two people in the place not drinking. Jane and Bartholomew seemed to be getting on famously. They were both talking animatedly, laughing and smiling and I risked a wry smile at the thought that Jane could really mess with some guys by pretending to be a girl only to reveal what was under her dress later on.

Big Ben and I made conversation to pass the time. It was nice to actually talk to him without him trying to get me into bed for once. Being out in a bar with him only made me think of Brett though and my need to speak with him to clear up the mess. He had asked me not to call though, so I wouldn't, even though I worried he would just meet someone while he was on his kitesurfing break. He was too handsome not to attract whatever females were in his location. What if he was in bed with one right now? Forgetting all about me as he writhed around with another girl.

Big Ben spoke to break my train of thought, 'You are having an odd effect.' I looked at him with a quizzical expression, so he would expand on his statement. 'When I go in a bar, girls come up to me. Doesn't matter if I'm already with a girl or if the girl coming over to me is out with her boyfriend or husband. Since we came in, not one girl has approached me, but I have had several smiles from different guys. They think I'm gay. You must look more convincing from a distance.'

'I guess I do.' I checked my watch. It was nearly ten o'clock. Two hours had slipped by. I was getting tired, not to mention bored. I hadn't thought their date would go on this long, but just as I was thinking about how I could possibly cause the date to end, Jane stood up. Bartholomew did likewise, then helped her into her long, elegant winter coat and walked her to the door. As they went by us, I could hear him asking if he could walk her home. It sounded like he had already asked several times when she replied that it really wasn't necessary.

Before we came into the bar, we had all agreed that if

the date came to a natural conclusion, Jane would leave and head back to my place. I would follow her, and Big Ben would follow Bartholomew. Jane was outside now and walking away. We could see her through the windows. I couldn't leave to catch up with her though because Bartholomew was standing in the doorway with his phone in his hands, his fingers typing something to someone. A minute went by. I wanted to leave, but I dare not get too close to him in case he recognised me.

Thankfully, he slipped his phone into a pocket, zipped up his coat against the cool air outside and left. I got up.

'Let's go,' I said to Big Ben, although I was already leaving. I turned around to check our plan as I pushed the door open. 'I'll try to catch up with Jane. Meet me back at mine?' He nodded, and I saw his eyes flare at something ahead of me.

I turned to see what he was looking at and bumped straight into Bartholomew as he came back into the bar.

There was a moment where he was about to apologise and then he saw through my disguise.

'You,' he sneered. 'Stalking me now, are you? Now I really will have to teach you a lesson.' He made to grab for me but suddenly the hulking form of Big Ben was in between us.

'I think you should reconsider that idea,' Big Ben said calmly.

I moved to the side so that I could see around Big Ben at what Bartholomew was doing. He pulled a hand-stitched doll-looking thing from his pocket – a voodoo doll and grabbed for Big Ben's hair. Big Ben punched him in the mouth and Bartholomew went bowling back out into the street, straight into the doorman's legs, felling him like a tree.

'Sorry about that,' Big Ben said as he stepped over the tangle of bodies. He had hold of my arm to steer me along. I was going anyway. We left the scene, any thought of tailing Bartholomew abandoned.

After Jane's Date

Jane had gone around the corner and stepped into the darkened alcove of a shop to wait for us. She emerged into the streetlight as we approached.

'Hey, guys.' She was smiling.

'Hey, how'd it go?' I asked.

Jane sighed and sort of gave herself a hug as she grinned at the sky before fixing her gaze back on us. 'He is such a sweetie. If I were not already in a relationship…'

'Err, Jane you seem to have forgotten the bit about him being a crazed stalker that attacks ex-girlfriends with chemicals.'

'Yeah,' said Big Ben. 'What do you think he would do to you after he lifts your skirt for the first time and finds himself confronted by the last chicken in the butcher's shop?'

Jane pursed her lips at him. 'I didn't say I was going to do anything, did I?'

'Never mind that, Jane. What did he say? Were you able

to get him to talk about voodoo or drugs or being an outright criminal scumbag?'

'No, I wasn't,' she replied, her face taking on the dreamy look again. 'He told me he works with his mum and dad at their chemical business developing new products for various industries. He showed me a couple of new products that they have intellectual property rights for and said that was how his parents made their money. He goes to church every Sunday and sings in the choir, and he is just lovely. He wants to see me again tomorrow night. He said he would plan something and call me.' She locked eyes with me. 'I think you have the wrong man.'

'Really? How much gin did you have?'

'It has nothing to do with the gin. I just can't see how that sweet boy is involved in the things you have said.'

'You met the client, right?'

'Oh, yeah.'

I rolled my eyes. Bartholomew was a good actor or had created a convincing alter ego that he let the world see while he went about his nefarious activities. Tonight, was a bust.

'Let's call it a night, okay? Jane, I will be spending tomorrow tailing Bartholomew. If he is involved in the manufacture of crystal meth all I need to do is follow him and work out where he is doing it. There will be trucks to bring raw material in and other vehicles to take the product out. Plus, he will need somewhere big to make it.'

Jane had nothing else to say on the matter, so we air kissed back at her car, and she went home. Big Ben waved us goodnight and jogged back towards the town, presumably to walk into a bar and pick up a girl for the night.

I went to bed.

Surveillance

I awoke in the dark. Disorientated for a moment, I remembered what I planned to do today and silently groaned to myself. Last night, when my ire was up, I had been determined that today I would follow Bartholomew wherever he went and prove that he was the Magdalene King. Now though, I admitted to myself that I had neither the skill nor the resource to pull something like that off.

Where the heck was Tempest when I needed him? He would know what to do and how to do it. As soon as the thought manifested, I pushed it back down. I rolled over and swung myself out of bed.

Stop being pathetic, Amanda. You don't need a man to rescue you.

I was going to be a strong woman. I was going to solve this for myself, not for anyone else – other than Kimberly, of course. I was going to be the master of my own destiny, dammit!

Yeah, but wouldn't it be nice if you married Brett and didn't have to do any of this?

The question that popped uninvited into my head had

my mother's voice. I ignored it as well and shoved an angry arm into my sports bra as I pulled it over my head. I was going to be the best version of me today. That started with doing some exercise. It would focus my mind and get me ready for the day.

I went out the door just after six o'clock. It was pitch dark and lightly drizzling, but I was going for a run and had Beyoncé in my ears to remind me how powerful I could be.

As she booted a man out of her life, because she could have another man in a minute, I turned away from my apartment and set off on the hard route, the one I really hated that made me run uphill.

Forty minutes later, I staggered back through the door to my place, out of breath, sweaty but elated. Today I was going to be a winner.

There were no spiders or snakes in my apartment. Perhaps the curse had a limited lifespan, or perhaps Bartholomew had bigger issues to attend to. I was going to find out what they were today. My first task was to go to Patience's place and see if she had come home yet. If she hadn't, then I needed to go to the station, or at least speak to them as her disappearance ought to now be something they were concerned about.

Breakfast was cream cheese and smoked salmon on a pair of bagels and a bowl of blueberries with natural yoghurt. Proud of myself for starting the day like a champion, I went out the door just after half past seven. The first stop on my list was Patience's building.

There was traffic on the roads already, plenty of it as busy people made their way to work and mums drove kids to school. It was moving though, so the drive to her building took no time at all.

Her car was still there in the same spot, but there were

no lights on in her apartment. I went up anyway and hammered on the door loudly enough to ensure she heard me if she was in and asleep, but not so loudly that I would wake all her neighbours.

I waited, but once again there was no response. Praying that she was just hooked up with a man somewhere, but not believing it for a minute, I trudged back out to my car and drove to the police station in the centre of town.

I didn't park in the car park around the back. I no longer had a pass to get me through the barrier. That had been taken from me as well. Instead, I parked in the visitors' car park like everyone else and had to put money in the ticket machine.

Manning the front desk was PC Alison French and Sgt Butterworth. I got on well with both.

Alison looked up and spotted me as I came through the front doors. 'Oh, hi, Amanda.'

Sgt Butterworth turned to see who it was, 'I didn't expect to see you back here so soon,' he said, peering over the top of his glasses.

'I just can't seem to stay away,' I replied, rather than get into why he thought I would want to avoid the place. I knew why: CI Quinn hated me and was determined to make my life horrible if he got a chance. 'I came to ask you about Patience, actually. I want to know if anyone has heard from her. She hasn't been home in two days and has abandoned her car and phone.'

Alison raised her eyebrows. Sgt Butterworth just tutted. He disliked Patience, with good reason as she was a bitch to him. To be fair Patience was horrible to most men, but some took it well and gave it back as good as they got, others, like Sgt Butterworth, took offence.

'Have you spoken with her family at all?' Alison asked.

'Yes, they don't know where she is. Her sister suggested she might just be with a man somewhere, but I don't think she is.'

'Why is that?' asked Sgt Butterworth, making no effort to conceal the disdain and boredom in his voice.

'Because she tells me everything. If there was a man, I would know about it.'

He didn't bother to reply. He found some paperwork to shuffle instead. 'Look,' I said, addressing Alison. 'I know that officially you can't do anything about this yet, but I'm reporting that PC Woods is missing and may be in trouble.'

Behind Alison, Sgt Butterworth gave a quiet snort.

'I'll make a few calls,' Alison assured me.

'No, you won't,' Sgt Butterworth shot back. 'You will get on with your job. Miss Woods will report for duty when she is next on shift and be just as unpleasant as usual.' He turned to me. 'I suppose you think she has been taken by your voodoo priest?' he watched my expression. 'Yes, we all know about your crazy theories now that you work for Tempest Michaels. No doubt there is a spook behind every corner at that ridiculous firm. You can see yourself out.'

I was being dismissed. One of their own was missing and might be hurt and I was being dismissed.

Alison flared her eyes at me. She was going to do what she could, no matter what Sgt Butterworth said. I heard Quinn's voice echoing through to the front desk from somewhere deeper in the station and decided it was time to leave.

I had to find Bartholomew and let him lead me to the crystal meth. I didn't know where he was though, and I couldn't afford to have him spot me tailing him. I had seen his car. If I had friends in the station still, I would be able to get them to look out for it, but I had the feeling that a request for help from me would be less well received than it would have been a few days ago. Quinn had probably threatened them all with disciplinary proceedings if they did help me.

I dismissed the notion of even asking and set off to see if I could find him myself. If I was a drug baron, chemical expert, stalker and fake voodoo priest, where would I be? I decided I would just have to go through a process of elimination and hope for the best. Reluctantly, I pointed the car in the direction of the Magdalene Estate and set off.

Terrance and Trevor

Wishing I had a different car because I was worried mine would be easily spotted, I cruised by Mason's house looking for Bartholomew, or at least for Bartholomew's car. I was once again keeping my eyes peeled for Terrance and Trevor and any of their friends.

There were a few people on the street, but the light drizzle had turned into a more persistent rain, typical of this time of year and it was keeping most people inside.

I drove around for a bit, checking the area, but decided I was probably safe so found a place to park that afforded me a good view of Mason's house. I didn't have much of a plan, I admitted. I was going to watch Mason's house for a while and if nothing happened, I would drive to Bearsted and see if Bartholomew turned up there. Sooner or later, he had to show up somewhere. I got the impression he wasn't afraid of being caught, that he considered it unlikely and that his parents would swiftly deploy the legal team to get him out of trouble anyway.

Ten minutes went by, which slowly turned into twenty

and my bum began to get numb from the lack of movement. I had to keep flicking the wipers on so that I could see the house. I worried it would draw attention to the stationary car but kept telling myself I was just being paranoid.

At 1053hrs, according to the little clock in my Mini I heard the familiar rumble of a tuned car. A few seconds later, Bartholomew's Japanese low-slung beast came into view. It parked in the street right outside Mason's house. I had never seen Mason, but a second person got out of the car from the passenger's side with keys to open the house. Bartholomew levered the back seat forward so that an elegant young woman with coffee-coloured skin could exit. He held her hand as she went with him to the house, trailing behind Mason.

I continued watching. One hand hovering over the ignition switch so I was ready to go when he came back out.

I was so focused on the front of the house that I missed Terrance and Trevor sneaking up on me. Just as the front door of the house opened again, so did my car door.

'Hey, bitch. All alone?' Trevor asked as he reached into my car and grabbed a handful of my hair. Bartholomew was just getting back into his car, and I needed to go. This is what I had been waiting for.

Rather than follow the instinctive move and pull against the hand in my hair, I threw myself toward it. It sent Trevor off balance, but he didn't let go of my hair. He was still off balance and not in control though as he stumbled, so I grabbed his wrist and twisted it against itself. Terrance was moving in to kick me, but with Trevor's right arm now mine to control, I pulled him into Terrance's path and the swinging boot hit Trevor in the head.

There was a string of swear words from both of them

and I spotted blood on the pavement. It was coming from Trevor's eyebrow. He was holding his head. Terrance's attention was on his friend. I could just dive in my car and get after Bartholomew. He had only just pulled away. I would catch up to him in no time.

I went for it, but as I grabbed the roof of my car to swing into my car seat, I changed my mind. I was bored with Trevor and Terrance. Trevor had his back to me, he was bent over, and Terrance was looking at his face where he had kicked it. I lined up and kicked Trevor square in the balls from behind. His head shot forward and up, connecting with Terrance's nose, which exploded across his face. Trevor was in shock, but the pain did not appear to have hit him yet. I kicked him again, this time in the arse and he tumbled to the ground.

Now I was done.

The House on the Green, Bearsted

I caught up with Bartholomew's Nissan GTR before he made it out of the Magdalene Estate. He was heading for Bearsted. I kept myself two cars back as we weaved through Maidstone, but when he turned off the main road and into Bearsted, I had to guess where he was going and drop back for fear of being seen. Way ahead of me, he turned again, this time taking a side turn just after the Green. He was going to his parent's house.

Then it hit me. His parents were in on it.

I checked my thinking. Did it make sense? They were so nice, so placid, but what if they had been criminals all along?

OMFG! What if Mr King was the original Magdalene King? The timeline made perfect sense. They were chemical experts, he was old enough to have created the legend thirty or more years back, and now Bartholomew was growing up to ... What? To take over? To be the new face of the criminal empire?

But was I wholly wrong? Maybe the parents were just

chemists. I couldn't take my suspicions to the police. CI Quinn would laugh me out of the station. Then, as I was trying to tell myself that I was probably wrong I remembered the door in the corner of their office. The one with stairs going down. I had thought at the time that it might be a wine cellar, but now I was willing to bet that it was a meth lab. Dozens of worker bees down there sweating in the heat as they cooked up drugs to sell to weak-willed individuals.

Suddenly, I was convinced that they were cooking the crystal meth in the lab at their house. I had seen a chemical delivery van leaving their place. They could use their business, fake or otherwise, as a front. I parked my car adjacent to the Green and went on foot.

Tracking across the grass, but sticking to the buildings that bordered the Green, I thought about the house I was heading for. It was massive, with a large extension on the back that they had designed. I needed to find a way to get a look inside the bits of the house I hadn't seen, especially the bit at the back.

I slunk along the wall of the property next door to sidle up next to the fence that was the edge of their property. I was trying to not be noticed by the persons inside the Kings' house, while at the same time hoping that I did not look like I was conspicuously sidling along the pavement trying to not be noticed by any casual observers looking out of their windows anywhere else in the village. I would need to slip inside the grounds and get a look through some windows. I was hoping I would find somewhere around the back where there was a way to see into the underground lab I was convinced existed.

I stopped at the edge of the property and searched for CCTV cameras that might be monitored inside. The rain was still a steady drizzle that had already soaked my hair and was now beginning to drip down my neck.

For a full minute, I watched the property for signs of movement.

Nothing.

Bartholomew's car was visible, its back end sticking out beyond a wall at the back of the house where I presumed he had parked near to a door. I clambered over the fence and hugged the tree line that bordered their property, then dashed across the open expanse of the driveway to reach the brickwork of the house. The gravel was noisy beneath my feet, but the rain created background noise to lessen the starkness of my movement. The rain was gurgling in gutters and downpipes and dripping in several places where it overflowed to drip, drip, drip onto the gravel many feet below.

I checked behind me once more and set off toward the back of the building. When I had gone inside the first time, Mrs King had taken me all the way to the lab which I believed was at the back of the building. I had become quite disorientated, so it was hard to tell, but she had said it was in the new part of the house they had added, and I hoped it would be obvious which bit that was when I got there.

At the corner of the house, I peered around carefully, not wanting to be seen by anyone that might be outside. There was no one there but along the back of the house, there were lots of windows. If anyone was inside the rooms at the back, they would see me. I checked behind me yet again, my heartbeat demanding I prove to it that I wasn't about to get caught, then I got on my hands and knees to crawl along the back of the house beneath the windows. My clothes were soaked and possibly wrecked from my efforts.

It wouldn't matter if I was right.

Jutting out perpendicular from the original house, was

an extension that must have been almost one hundred feet long. I couldn't see how wide it was, but it stretched at least a third of the width of the house and was about one and a half floors tall. I imagined inside it had a vaulted ceiling, so it housed the office Mrs King had taken me to and inside would be the staircase that led down.

There were windows all along this side of the extension where the corridor inside ran along the wall and all the rooms came off the other side of it. I couldn't see anything that indicated a cellar. No ventilation outlet or window in the floor to let in light. Maybe there would be around the other side as I could also not see where a delivery van would collect and deliver goods/products. There was no way I could get along the extension without people in the house seeing me run down the garden. I would have to go back and try to get to the other side of the extension by going all the way around the front of the house.

I turned around and my heart almost came out of my chest. Bartholomew was behind me. He was pointing a taser gun at me. My brain raced as I tried to think of something to say. I didn't have to though because he smiled and pulled the trigger.

Wonderful Diversity

Someone was touching me. No, something was touching me. It was an object, not a person. It felt more like a wet brush than skin. It was cold rather than warm.

I slowly forced my heavy eyes open and my head up. Why did I have to lift my head up? It took a second before all the information that was being relayed to my brain sorted itself into order. I was in a darkened room lit by candles, and I was tied to an upright gurney of some kind. It felt like it was made of wood as it wasn't cold against my skin like metal would be. I glanced down to confirm I was right. It looked to be hewn from the branches of a tree and lashed together with string. This wasn't the most alarming concern though.

I was naked.

The fact that all my clothes had been removed ought to be alarming enough, but it was entirely secondary in my list of worries to the half-dozen other naked women in the room. All African or Caribbean descent, their skin was painted with odd patterns from head to toe. They all looked to be in a trance-like state, and they were using the same paint on me – the wet brush had woken me.

The two women that were painting me moved to the side as two more stepped up with different paint. One of them was Patience!

'Patience!' I hissed to get her to look at me. She was focused on the task of painting me and didn't even react. 'Patience,' I tried again. My arms were restrained so I couldn't touch her or grab her. I could barely move at all, and the bonds dug into my skin painfully as I tried to struggle against them.

Patience had the same faraway look as the other five women. Whether they were drugged or hypnotised or something else I couldn't tell but they were all non-responsive. Patience finished painting my left arm and was replaced by the next woman in line. It seemed they were done with the painting as the next two had long necklaces made of bone to place over my head. The bones looked like they might be those of a human finger, and they didn't look clean - like there might still be scraps of flesh stuck to them.

It was quite horrific, my senses almost at overload point and threatening to send me into a tailspin of panic that would render me incapable of rational thought. I needed to be able to think if I was going to escape this. I thought back to my earlier annoyance over weak thoughts of having someone rescue me. Rescue, though, was looking like a favourable outcome now.

The women turned away and began filing from the room.

'Patience,' I called after her before she could leave the room. 'Patience!' The last one I shouted out loud, but there was no reaction from her at all.

As the last woman left the room, Bartholomew appeared

in the doorway. He was wearing a robe that had no arms and a pair of loose-fitting trousers that matched the material of the robe. Both garments were colourfully embroidered. His body was painted in a different pattern to the women that had just left and looked more like his skeleton was sitting outside his skin. It was the same effect I had seen on Halloween.

'I did say I would make her my slave.' He laughed deeply as if it was really funny then stood and stared at my naked body, taking it all in.

'You won't get away with this.' It was all I could think of to say. It sounded so cliched to my ears. He simply smiled at me. 'People know where I was heading today,' I lied, trying to keep my voice from cracking. 'They will come for me soon enough.' I was trying to sound confident, but he laughed again.

'Do you mean your big friend? He turned up a while ago looking for you. He clearly didn't know all that much about our operation, although I will say that he displayed a fairly iron will in resisting our torture methods.'

Oh no! They had Big Ben!

'In the end, it was clear that he didn't know anything, but I had them carry on for a while just in case.'

'What did you do to him?' I demanded, anger replacing my fear now.

'Oh, I don't think you should worry too much about him. He will be dead soon enough. You should worry about your own limited future. Soon the ladies will return for you, and you will join me at my wedding. You see, you're to be a glorious honour sacrifice. Your blood will make me more powerful yet.'

He was planning to murder me. I was beyond terrified.

Without ropes to hold me up I swear I would have collapsed.

He took a step forward and leaned in, so his face was mere inches from mine, 'The ceremony also requires a ritualistic rape before the victim is murdered.' My breath caught with the horror of what I was hearing. 'Don't worry though, we have someone else for that. No such indignity for you. You get to die from dozens of venomous snake bites.'

He spun on his feet and went back out the door. 'See you soon, Miss Harper.' His voice echoed back down the hallway outside.

I was alone. I was utterly terrified, and I was alone. No one knew where I was, and I couldn't see how anyone would find me. For that matter, I didn't know where I was either. Had I been transported somewhere while I was unconscious? Or was I somewhere in the basement of the Kings' house? Would my body ever be found?

I struggled against the ropes that held me again. I could feel them tearing at my skin. They didn't give though. Not one little bit.

I looked around the room wondering if I could find something, a tool I could reach. I tried rocking the gurney I was strapped to. It moved a little. If I could just wobble my way across the room to the shelf I could see, maybe there would be something there I could use.

The thought died on my brow though as the catatonic ladies filed back into the room followed by Mrs King. She wore a dress and robe that exposed huge amounts of her flesh. It was split down the centre to reveal her breasts which wobbled rhythmically with each stride.

'So good of you to join us, Miss Harper. We would have

found someone to fulfil your role easily enough, but to volunteer in the manner that you did was truly inspiring.'

'Why are you doing this?' I managed to stammer out.

'Why?' she asked as if it should be obvious. 'Because practising voodoo is the source of our power. My husband and I rose from nothing through a campaign of utter terror. Why work hard for a living when you can trap the souls of your rivals or control them through fear? You think we could have afforded all this by being chemists?'

'You make crystal meth, don't you?'

'Among other things, yes. Why wouldn't we? Voodoo makes us strong and crystal meth makes others weak. They are so dependent upon us, so ready to obey our demands. Come now, enough chatter.' She clapped her hands and the six women, Patience included, surrounded the gurney, tilted it backward so I faced the ceiling and lifted it from the floor.

'Patience what are you doing? Get me out of here,' I wailed. I worried I might lose control of my bladder I was that scared of what was coming.

Patience did not respond though. Neither did anyone else as they carried me out of the room and down the dark corridor. We turned a corner, and the tone of noise changed just before we entered a huge chamber. It must have been three stories high, like being inside a cathedral. I was straining my head to see where I was being taken and what was around me. It was hard to make much out, the chamber was lit by thousands of candles which created shadows everywhere, but ahead of me, as I stared through my feet, there was an altar of sorts. The noise I had heard before, which had started out as nothing more than a quiet susurration in the background turned out to be chanting from dozens of people. They were wearing scraps of clothing and were swaying as they chanted.

Mr King was standing next to the altar. In contrast to everyone around him, his skin wasn't painted. He had on a top hat and tails, plus trousers, but no shirt, leaving his chest exposed. In his right hand, he held a cane, the ball on top was a small human skull. I suspected it was real. Around his neck was a large black snake. I could see it moving.

On the stone floor, by Mr King's feet was the bloody and naked body of Big Ben. I couldn't tell if he was alive or dead, but he wasn't moving and looked to have taken a beating. How many of them had it taken to capture him I wondered?

My gurney stopped moving and was standing upright again. Mr King descended steps that led down from the altar. He had the snakes head in his hand.

'Welcome, Miss Harper,' he said as if I was just arriving for a cocktail party. He brushed the snake's head against my face. One side, then the other, and then held it in front of my face. If he was trying to terrify me, he needn't have bothered, I was so far past the point of terror it was getting laughable. The snake's tongue flicked out, kissing the tip of my nose. Mr King laughed a deep belly laugh.

'Come now,' he called to the audience. 'Let us begin.'

Something was pressed into my hand. The movement came from behind me and was urgent as if the person doing it had to be quick about what they were doing. I was still strapped onto my gurney and couldn't see who it had been. I risked a glance down.

It was a small knife, barely an inch long and with a tiny double-edged blade.

The six naked women walked in front of me, taking up position three on each side. Patience was to my left. Did I see her move? Did she just twitch? I watched and just when

I thought I had imagined it, her right hand moved again. Behind her back, she gave me a thumbs up.

Patience was with me! I wasn't alone. I almost sobbed as hope filled my chest. Then I thought about the knife and wondered where Patience had been hiding it. It felt moist. I told myself it was sweat and decided I would be happier not finding out if I was right or wrong.

In front of the altar, Mr King began a chant. The words were gibberish to me. He pulled the large black snake from around his neck, holding it just below its head, he held it aloft by one hand. The crowd of people that edged the room were swaying to the rhythm of his words. It might have been in Haitian or any other language that I did not understand.

Mrs King joined him at the altar, her boobs swinging as she walked and there were two bare-chested men following her while carrying a large basket between them. It was almost person size and looked to be three feet deep. I didn't want to think about what might be in it. I didn't have to guess for long though as Mrs King reached in to pluck out two snakes. They were small and had bands of red, yellow and black running the length of their body. I knew almost nothing about snakes but still knew enough to be certain these ones were deadly.

'Let us anoint our sacrifices,' Mr King's voice boomed. Then he held the large black snake aloft and cut off its head. The snake's writhing ceased instantly but Mr King was moving it himself as he flicked the severed end at Big Ben to splash fresh blood on his back. Then he crossed the floor to me and did the same. Warm liquid hit the skin of my face and chest and ran down over my belly. I was so disgusted I wanted to vomit. Had there been any food in me I probably would have.

Slowly, I had turned the knife around in my hand to rest it on the twine holding me in place. I moved it against the tension of my restraint convinced I would drop the blade at any moment. Instead, I felt the binding loosen as something gave.

From an unseen portal behind the altar, Bartholomew emerged with the girl I had seen him with earlier just behind him. Behind them came Mason, I recognised him from earlier but then in contrast to all the dark-skinned, black-haired people, the next person was a tall, thin blonde woman in a dress.

It was Jane.

'Now brethren,' Mr King addressed the room, his deep voice booming. 'It is time for the culmination of our wedding celebrations. Our annual sacrifice will this year not be one but three individuals. Their blood will stoke our power. We will rule over our rivals, subjugating them with our drugs as we exploit their weakness. Voodoo will guide our actions and terrify all who would challenge us. You, loyal servants of the Magdalene King, you will flourish with me and share in my riches.'

My ears had not deceived me. I had worked it all out. It wasn't Bartholomew that was the Magdalene King, it was his dad. The timeline worked, but I had figured it out too late to tell anyone. The chance of exposing them felt slim given my current predicament. However, my right hand was now loose enough for me to slide it out of the remaining loops of string. I dare not move to cut my other bindings though for fear I would be spotted. I needed a distraction.

Two large, bare-chested, muscular men were holding Jane in place. They had forced her to her knees, and each had one meaty hand on her shoulders. In the hand that wasn't holding her, each had a large knife which might more accurately be described as a short sword. Jane looked terrified but did not appear to be hurt.

The young woman I had seen with Bartholomew stepped in front of Mr King leading Bartholomew by his hand. 'Now my prince, take this young woman. Celebrate the end of your life as a single man, give her your seed then kill her and join with me forever as my husband.' She took his shoulders and turned him to face Jane.

I suddenly realised that Jane was the one he was planning to publicly rape as part of his twisted ritual.

They didn't know it was a man beneath the makeup and dress. This should be good.

Bartholomew took a pace towards Jane. There was a maniacal look on his face. His excitement was clear, not only in his smile but also in the bulge jutting out from the front of his pants. His bride to be grasped his robe and pulled it from his shoulders.

The two men holding Jane in place lifted her to her feet then one used his enormous blade to slice the back of her dress. It fell away, taking her fake boobs with it and revealing the meat and two veg hanging between his legs just as Bartholomew pulled the cord that held up his trousers and let them fell the floor.

In the sudden silence of the room, all eyes were on Jane. Mr King's eyes were popping out his head in disbelief that the blonde girl had a penis. Then Patience laughed.

It was a cackling snort of suppressed laughter like she was trying not to but couldn't contain it. I knew what she was laughing at, Bartholomew had a tiny penis, and she was pointing at it. All eyes swung to her. Mr and Mrs King's faces were incredulous. Their plan for the ceremony was unravelling fast. Bartholomew looked down at his tiny winky and across at Jane's much larger version, his expression horrified. His erection was already beginning to wilt.

If I had been viewing this scene from a safe distance, I might have enjoyed it. As it was, I was still about to be murdered and needed to rescue myself. I took the brief opportunity I was given and with a single slash of the blade, I cut the bonds of my left hand and then my feet. The knife was sharp, and my fast movements nicked my skin. I was free though and I had a weapon.

Simultaneous with me gaining freedom, Big Ben came back to life. I missed it because I was cutting myself free and I didn't see him hit Mr King, but I heard the outrush of air from Mr King's lungs and Mrs King's screech of outrage.

By the time I looked up, Mr King was tumbling to the floor, and Big Ben was rushing the two men holding Jane. Caught by indecision, one didn't move at all, choosing instead to keep hold of Jane and use her as a shield, the other twitched, realised the danger approaching and moved to intercept Big Ben with his weapon. Too late though, Big Ben closed the distance before the man could raise his knife and struck him with a haymaker right fist that felled him like a tree.

Mrs King and Bartholomew's bride were going for Patience. The other five naked women – shall we call them bridesmaids? They hadn't moved. They were still trapped in the trancelike state Patience had been faking. Patience saw the danger coming. She was more than capable of smacking down two skinny bitches, but the growing hope for escape I was beginning to feel, ended when I saw the audience begin to move in. There were four of us and over fifty of them. Big Ben might take out a dozen of them, maybe more but the numbers were insurmountable in my head. In seconds they would be upon us. I needed a way out.

Maybe the hidden entrance that Bartholomew had come through. I didn't know if it led out of the building, but I had to try. There was no one near me. No one I needed to fight my way through.

'Patience!' I yelled as she grabbed Mrs King and upended her. The smaller lady flipped in the air before Patience smashed her skull into the floor. Patience slammed into the bride in a body check that knocked her flying. Then she was running after me. Big Ben and Jane were ahead of us. I glanced at Patience and wished I hadn't. She was naked and had boobs that, without the benefit of support, and with the addition of frantic motion, had turned into an additional pair of limbs. They were going different directions so that her nipples were now about three feet apart. Of all the images my eyes had captured tonight, this was perhaps the one that would stay with me the longest.

The man holding Jane had seen his colleague easily beaten by the giant, muscular, naked, white man and switched his tactic as he put his blade to Jane's throat. Jane was too light to fight him off and was clearly panicked, hanging loose in the man's grip.

All three of us skidded to a halt. We couldn't leave, and we couldn't overpower him without him cutting Jane's throat first.

'Enough!' roared Mr King. He'd regained his feet and was helping his wife up. Just in front of him, Bartholomew was putting his trousers back on. 'You will all die for your insolence.' The audience has moved from their positions at the edge of the room but hadn't fully closed the distance, they were surrounding the central Dais that we, the Kings and the altar were on. Their numbers formed a tight circle around the four of us. There was nowhere to go and many of them were armed while we were not.

Mr King stepped forward, nodding to someone behind us as he did. The man holding Jane let her go but rushed forward to put his knife to Big Ben's neck instead. He was joined by others. Big Ben was the threat, and everyone knew it. The sweet, little blonde girl wasn't.

The danger of Big Ben now effectively neutralised, Mr King took control of proceedings once more. He stepped around the large wicker basket full of snakes, brushed by his son and came to me. He held out his right hand to his side. A lacky placed a wicked looking blade into it. Then he held out his left hand to me.

I looked at it dumbly. He motioned with his fingers for me to step forward. I saw no choice.

'Amanda?' Patience wailed as I moved toward him. She was as terrified as I. What could I do though? I was just a woman. A poor, defenceless woman. Concealed in my hand, no one had seen the knife I still held.

Mr King continued to address the crowd, 'My people. Let us celebrate this night anyway. Fresh sacrifices will be found, and we will hold the wedding ceremony soon.' He lifted his knife above his head. He was watching the crowd, raising them to a clamouring fervour as they begged for blood. Then, he turned his eyes in my direction and reached out to grab me. I lunged and stabbed him in the throat with my tiny blade.

Until that moment I wasn't sure I could do it. I was terrified almost beyond the capacity for rational thought. I was ready to pee myself, but somehow, I was also angry. Angry that Big Ben was considered to be a threat and I wasn't. Angry that they had dismissed me as defenceless. Angry that I was wishing someone, even a man, would come to my rescue. I doubted that injuring Mr King would aid my cause, but he deserved it, and I was damned if I was going to meekly let him kill me.

Stunned by the blow to his throat, he froze, his left-hand letting go its grip on my arm. He coughed once, blood visible on his lips, then before anyone could react, I kicked him in his spuds and shoved him backward into the basket of snakes.

That'll teach him!

Mrs King screamed, her mouth a horrified circle of disbelief. Mr King thrashed for a few seconds as the snakes attacked the sudden weight pressing down on them, then lay still, my blade still sticking out of his throat.

'Aaaargggh!' screamed Bartholomew as he grabbed the knife his father had dropped and ran at me.

He never made it though. As he took his first step in my direction his right shoulder exploded. One moment it was there and the next it wasn't. The deafening sound of a gunshot followed a nanosecond later to tell us what was going on and my heart skipped as I saw black uniforms spilling into the room.

Shouted orders were being barked as armed police swarmed into the crowd before they could work out what was going on. The voodoo disciples were being thrown to the floor with weapons trained on them, daring them to resist.

Big Ben seized his chance, elbowed the man behind him hard in the face, took his weapon and then moved to make sure no one escaped down the passage behind the altar. Wherever it went, no one was going to get by the angry giant guarding it now.

I grabbed Jane by the arm, pulled her toward me and put a protective arm around Patience. Big Ben, Jane and I stood out as the only white people in the room, but Patience looked like all the other crazed voodoo buttholes. I didn't want the armed officers to seize her in their desire to make the room safe.

'Amanda!'

The call brought my face up. It was Tempest. He'd come in behind the uniforms. He was unarmed and wearing civilian clothes. He looked tired and a little beaten like he'd endured a hard week. I was willing to bet I could top whatever fun he had in Cornwall.

'Amanda!' he called again as he made his way across the room. The police were dealing with the voodoo crazies and were leaving us alone. They would get to us soon enough.

As Tempest neared, I saw CI Quinn enter the room behind him. No doubt this would be recorded as his bust now. To hell with it, I was just glad to be alive.

Tempest reached the central dais. 'Amanda … oh, ah, you don't seem to be wearing very much.' Tempest was looking at the ceiling in a bid to not stare at me.

I had been naked for so long and surrounded by so many naked people that I had forgotten my lack of clothing.

'Um, none of you do, actually,' he said taking in Big Ben, Jane, and Patience.

He turned around. 'Can we get some clothing over here, please?'

Press Conference

About half an hour later, I was sitting on a blanket with another blanket around me. Hot tea and bacon sandwiches had been rustled up from somewhere and I had on bits and pieces of clothing that different people had given up. Tempests' jacket, some spare police boots from the back of squad car. A pair of slightly smelly jogging bottoms from a gym bag. I was covered though and that was good enough. They had found Patience's clothes and Big Ben's and Jane had used some duct tape to stick her dress back together. The clothes I had arrived in were still missing.

We were still in the chamber under the house. CI Quinn was coordinating all movement in and out, or at least he had several officers that were doing that for him. I expected that soon we would be given the all-clear to leave by the paramedics that were currently checking over Big Ben, and they would want us out of the way.

The voodoo community was already gone. Every last one of them had been led in handcuffs out through the entrance the police had burst in through, even the five drugged up naked girls. The only exception to that had been the Kings. Mr King was pronounced very dead at the scene by an efficient-looking doctor that came with the paramedics. Bartholomew had needed treatment for pain and to stop the blood loss as the bullet that went through his shoulder had made a real mess and broken some bones on its way. Mrs King, having seen her husband die, her son get shot, and her entire criminal world come tumbling down, had retreated into a state of shock. She had left on a stretcher. Handcuffed, but on a stretcher, nevertheless.

I finished my tea and set the cup down on the floor next to me.

'The press are here,' someone said, their voice echoing in the underground room. My eyes found Quinn. He was instantly straightening his tie and checking to make sure his uniform looked good. I wondered if the Chief Constable was on his way.

'How are you doing?' the voice was Tempest's. I turned to where it had come from. He was checking on Big Ben and talking with the paramedics. They clearly wanted Big Ben to go to the hospital with them. He was laughing at them and shaking his head. Next to him, and holding his hand, was Patience. They had both been through a lot, maybe they would find comfort in each other.

Or maybe they both just fancied a shag, and it was too late in the day to find anyone else.

Tempest nodded, chucked Big Ben on the shoulder with a fist and crossed the floor to me.

I had a question for him, 'How did you find me?' We hadn't yet had any chance to talk since the police had swooped in. I had been struggling with several emotions ever since. Relief at seeing him. Even more relief that I wasn't going to be bitten to death by snakes but then anger that I had been rescued when I specifically wanted to rescue myself and not have a man save me like I was a damned damsel in distress. I was also curious about what his week in Cornwall had been like. He wore outdoor clothing, the type one might wear for hill walking or rock climbing, but it was dirty as if he'd been fighting. His knuckles were bruised and cut in places and there were several faint marks on his face.

The dominant thought though was how he came to find me. Even I didn't know where I was. Or at least I hadn't. Big Ben had told me that we were still on the Kings' property, somewhere deep beneath their house.

In answer to my question, he said, 'Your car.'

I wondered what he meant for a moment, then remembered that I had left it outside someone's house. Like most villages, parking was at a premium so parking without a permit was limited to two hours. I hadn't expected to be that long when I parked it.

'I went to the station and made a lot of noise until they checked to see where your cars were. They had squad cars do a drive by everyone's properties. Patience's car was at her house, Jane's was at hers, but I called her house phone and got a tearful Simon explaining that she was missing. Both your car and Big Ben's had been towed from close to here. It took a little doing and I had to have a word with our friend Quinn where I made it clear I would expose his deliberate lack of effort if he didn't get off his butt and act. One of the other Officers whispered that you had reported Patience missing already and it was being largely ignored.'

He'd saved me. He'd driven back from the other side of the country, coerced a senior police officer who hated him into taking action, found me, and had genuinely saved the day. I felt like kissing him. I also felt like berating him for saving me, but I knew that my anger really should be focused inwards. I should have told Jane where I was going, I should have been better prepared. I should have done something to save myself.

Instead, I stood up and gave him a hug. He stiffened, unsure how to react or where to put his hands. I liked that about him. He's quite awkward around me in a way that he isn't with anyone else.

As I broke the hug, he quickly found something to talk about, 'Did you get a chance to speak to Patience? Find out how she got here?'

I nodded, then I told him about it. She had answered a knock on her door late on Tuesday evening and had been tasered the second she opened it. After that, she didn't remember much else and suspected they had given her Rohypnol or another, similar narcotic that could have induced the confused and compliant state she found herself in. Like me, she'd woken up naked but hadn't really noticed until the drug had finally started wearing off earlier today. By then she was in a group of other women, all naked and being given instructions. She played along, hoping a chance to escape would arise but she did not know where she was, and it was only just before she saw me that she first saw Mrs King and understood who had taken her.

There had been a flurry of activity many hours before she was led into the chamber where I was held, she was trying to judge time without a clock or daylight as a reference and struggling to work out how long it had been. I had been tasered around noon and it was after midnight when Tempest arrived with the police. I had been out for half a day, and they had kept Patience captive for more than two. Patience said she had tried whispering to the other girls, they didn't respond, even when she poked them. Whatever drug they had used to create the catatonic state was good stuff. No doubt the hospital would work out what it was later.

She'd seen the Kings and lots of men with weapons and a basket of snakes and lots and lots of voodoo shit (her words not mine) and had freaked out so much that by the time she was instructed to paint me for the ceremony she'd withdrawn into herself and was numbly doing what she was told. The knife, she said, had been on a shelf in the chamber I was being held in. She had spontaneously grabbed it in passing and stashed it in something I hadn't heard because I had seen the awful answer coming and had put my fingers in my ears while making a, 'La, la, la,' sound to block out what she was saying.

I had also spoken with Big Ben while Tempest had been off coordinating with the police. He didn't want to talk about his treatment at the hands of the Kings. All he would say was that he got a call from Jane to say that Patience had gone missing and then she couldn't get hold of me and he started snooping. The first place he went was the Kings' house. It was after dark. He broke into the house and was overpowered. He didn't have much more than that to say about it.

'Ben doesn't do emotions,' Tempest said. 'He will deal with it in his own way.'

It seemed impolite to not ask him about his week away. 'Jane said you had her looking into pirate ships and treasure while you were away. I thought you were taking some time off to relax.'

He followed my gaze down to his ripped and dirty clothing. He laughed at himself, 'It, ah… It turned out to be more adventurous than I had intended. I'll tell you about it later if you like. Shall we check on the others?'

Tempest and I walked the few feet over to where Big

Ben, Patience, and Jane were waiting impatiently. The police had been kind and caring, we were the victims after all, but they didn't or rather couldn't let us go until they had assessed enough of the crime scene and asked a few questions. That had already happened while the paramedics had been checking each of us over.

Jane had called her boyfriend, Simon just as soon as she could get hold of a phone. He'd reported her absence to the police last night, the only one of us that was reported missing. Not enough time had elapsed for the police to investigate it yet though. He'd arrived twenty minutes ago and was waiting somewhere outside, so Jane was getting quite agitated at being made to hang around. The police trauma management rep had given Jane and the rest of us the number for a counsellor we could talk to. Big Ben had laughed and thrown it away. Patience and I had been more polite about it. I didn't know if I would have nightmares about today, about Bartholomew. It wasn't something I wanted to think about now.

A few more minutes went by while we waited, doing nothing, amid the flurry of activity that surrounded us, and just when I decided I had had enough, a sergeant detached himself from a group that was setting up a small operations post and came to tell us we were free to go.

I thanked him and turned to make sure everyone was ready. 'Let's get the heck out of here.' Everyone agreed with the sentiment.

On the way out, we met with more police and more crime scene guys in the corridors. Beneath the Kings' house was chemical storage, a meth lab, and goodness knows what else. As I went by one room, I saw Simon and Steve in the distance. White lab suits on, they were inspecting what I took to be chemistry equipment. Seeing them made me remember Kimberly. I would need to call and update her. She would want to know that Bartholomew was gone and wouldn't be coming back. I wouldn't need her toiletries anymore either. No one would be interested in prosecuting a stalker case when he was going down for drug manufacture and distribution and quite possibly murder – how many other people had been snatched and sacrificed over the years?

A thought occurred to me. 'Jane?' I had to turn my head and sort of walk sideways in the corridor, so I could see her. 'When they kidnapped you, did they say anything about their plans for you?' I had already asked her about how and when they had grabbed her. It had been as she got home on Thursday afternoon. Three of them had been waiting near her house and had bundled her into a van as she crossed the car park to her house.

Jane thought about my question for a moment. 'No. No, I don't think they did, other than to say that I was the lucky one. I did hear them talking when they thought I couldn't hear them. They said something about the girl they wanted disappearing and that Mr King was lucky to have found a replacement in the nick of time. Any idea what that means?'

Tempest put his hand on my shoulder to guide me around a pillar as I wasn't really watching where I was going.

'Thanks,' I mumbled, deep in thought. 'I think Bartholomew needed a girl for the ritual tonight. That's why he was using the dating site in the first place. Kimberly would have been the intended target or one of the previous girls, but I guess he always put out a creepy vibe and the girls all shied away. It should have been Kimberly tonight, but we stashed her out of their reach, and he grabbed you because you suddenly popped into his life.'

'That is seriously disturbing,' said Big Ben.

We emerged into the cool night air via a set of concrete steps that led up into a corner of the expansive garden. The rumble of generators powering portable lights could be heard coming from the front of the house. Light from there was creating long shadows. As we rounded the building the noise increased, and we could hear a single voice ahead of us.

CI Quinn was giving a press report. On the other side of the ornate garden fence, out in the street was a hastily erected podium with microphones attached to the front of it. A boom with a further microphone was being held above his head while three different cameras were trained on him.

As we closed the distance, I began to make out what he was saying.

'...together with armed officers, the building behind us was stormed at 0137hrs this morning. This follows a lengthy investigation by my department into the Magdalene King and the supply of drugs in this area.' He was a good orator and played well to the camera. I had seen him on the news before. It was one of the skills that had gained him promotion already and would see him continue to rise. I loathed him.

This was my bust, and he was claiming it as his own.

'The arrests made here tonight will see a marked reduction in crime ...'

'Hey, it's Tempest Michaels!' One of the reporters shouted, grabbing her cameraman and pointing him right at us. CI Quinn's voice trailed off as he realised that all attention, and the cameras, had shifted away from him.

I heard Tempest say a bad word under his breath, but then he raised his arm and waved to the press as they came toward us. We had closed the last few metres and were exiting the grounds of the house to join the press in the street.

'Good evening,' he offered with enthusiasm. 'Would you like an eyewitness account of tonight's events?' he asked them.

'Mr Michaels, you're not required, thank you,' CI Quinn cut in loudly.

The press though was ignoring the man in uniform. They were focused on the rag-tag band of refugees with Tempest Michaels, local minor celebrity, in the centre. Tempest stepped onto the podium next to Quinn, offering the man his hand to shake for the cameras. Quinn returned the smile, failing to hide how false it looked as he took Tempest's hand.

The reporters were already shouting out questions. 'How did you become involved in the case? Is it true they were practising voodoo? Is voodoo real, Tempest?'

Moving to the centre of the podium, which bodily forced the smaller man in uniform to step aside, Tempest addressed the cameras. 'Thank you, Chief Inspector,' he said with a smile, then he speared the cameras with a serious look. 'The Kent Police were magnificent this evening, their bravery and determined action led to the successful arrest of an entire criminal organisation. There is an element the Chief Inspector is not aware of though.' He turned his gaze to me. The cameras followed it, and I was instantly pinned in place by several bright lights. 'My colleague, Amanda Harper investigated this case while I was absent. I have played no part in the apprehension of the Magdalene King; However, the Chief Inspector will confirm that Miss Harper was instrumental in bringing him to justice. Isn't that right, Chief Inspector?' The cameras swung back to Quinn.

'Well, I, ah ...'

Tempest didn't give him room to disagree. 'During her investigation into a related case, Miss Harper uncovered evidence that led her to believe she had identified the elusive criminal legend that you all know as the Magdalene King...'

'I think it's time I concluded my official report,' CI Quinn said, interrupting Tempest. Perhaps sensing the mood of the reporters, Tempest fell silent, allowing Quinn to speak. 'Now, where was I? Crime in this area will be greatly reduced, due solely...'

'We want to hear from Tempest and Harper!' a male reporter shouted.

'Yeah!' said the man next to him.

'This is an official statement to the press ...' Quinn tried. He employed his authoritative voice.

'Yeah, but you're boring,' pointed out someone.

'Let Tempest speak!' called out a young female reporter, shivering visibly against the cold.

Tempest shrugged and stepped back to the centre of the podium as CI Quinn spun angrily on his heels and left.

As Tempest talked, I watched him. He was being utterly selfless, talking about me in the most generous terms while at the same time verbally defeating a man I desperately wanted to see fail.

I jumped lightly as something touched my left calf. I looked down to find a small Persian cat wearing a Swarovski collar. It was Kimberly's cat. Bartholomew had taken it. I picked it up, surprised that it didn't fight me. It began purring as I rubbed its fur.

'Did you rescue her?' One of the reporters called out as Tempest was explaining his presence at the house.

'Not in any sense of the word, no,' he replied.

It felt like a lie to me. Had he not turned up I would be dead now.

'By the time the police arrived, Amanda had already escaped from captivity, overpowered Mr King and, together with her team,' he indicated Big Ben, Patience, and Jane, 'she would most likely have brought about the gang's surrender.'

There was a snort of derision from CI Quinn who was now standing to one side fuming.

I felt Patience next to me. She leaned in close to my ear and whispered, 'And remember that on top of all this adulation, he is also a little bit in love with you.'

My heart skipped. There was a lot to like about Tempest Michaels. Thinking about a non-professional relationship with him just made me think of Brett though. Where was Brett? Did getting kidnapped and nearly killed qualify as grounds to break my promise not to call him?

I was fairly sure it did. I would send him a text or an email telling him not to worry if he saw me on the news. That was bound to get a response even if it was a little manipulative.

I was going to win Brett back. Once he knew he'd misunderstood seeing me with Big Ben, I was sure we would be back on track. Tempest Michaels though …

Unconsciously I bit my lip as I watched him.

Sleep

Tempest had wrapped the press interview up, stating that we had all endured a very long day, had been subjected to harsh treatment and degradation and needed to attend to our own needs. They had pressed him with more questions, but he'd politely insisted that we were done for the night. There would be other opportunities to interview us.

His Dachshunds were in his two-seater sports car I learned as he made arrangements to get us home. He opened the door, and they plopped out to greet everyone with an excited round of barking. He shushed them and put them back inside, explaining that he'd come directly here from Cornwall and really needed to get them home. We told him to go, but of course, he insisted on staying until our transport home was fixed.

Jane had been reunited with her boyfriend who had been held behind the police cordon, and she vanished with Simon almost before we realised what was happening. Tempest called after her to take the next day off and to only come back next week when she was ready.

The rest of us went into the back of a police van, the kind used for transporting prisoners. None of us cared, it was just a means to get home. Patience should have been the first drop as her house was nearest but at some point, this evening she had negotiated a second date with Big Ben and was going to his place. How they had the energy to even consider sex I had no idea. I was exhausted.

I waved them both goodnight from the van as they were dropped in the street by the solid looking security gate that led into Big Ben's building complex. Tempest had told me to take tomorrow off as well. I suspected that I wouldn't wake up until late morning, but when I did, I would have tasks to perform. I had to reunite Kimberly with her cat for one. My sleep-deprived brain was telling me I had forgotten an important fact about her. Something I needed to do or something I needed to tell her. I couldn't work out what it was though and was certain it could wait until morning.

I needed a shower but elected to just put my sheets through the wash tomorrow instead. I was bone tired. My only concession, diverting my direct route from front door to bed, was to clean my teeth.

As I relaxed into my bed covers, Kimberly's cat curled up on one corner of my duvet, my phone rang. I picked it up to switch it off. It was far too late to consider answering it. The caller was Tempest, so I swiped the screen to connect him.

'Hi, Tempest.'

'Amanda why is there a woman in my bed?'

Oops!

vinci-books.com/witches-eastmalling

Tempest Michaels' office has burnt down, his love life is a joke and he's convinced he's getting fat. It's the perfect time for a new case then!

The client is the son of a man who was killed in a freak accident - struck by lightning. That doesn't sound very paranormal until you learn that he was inside his house when it happened and his heart exploded from his chest. There are eldritch runes drawn on the victim's house and his wife, together with several of her friends, has been seen colluding with a mysterious old crone.

Turn the page for a free preview…

The Witches of East Malling:
Chapter One

CAR CHASE

Friday, November 4th 1722hrs

I watched my knuckles turn white where they gripped the dashboard. I had both legs braced against the forward bulkhead of the car, the bit that separates the cockpit from the engine bay, knowing even as I did, that doing so meant I would most likely break them both if we did crash.

'Hang on!' yelled Jagjit as he flung the steering wheel around. The car was right on the edge of its ability, the tyres screeching their complaint as they struggled for grip amid competing forces, some trying to propel the car forward, some trying to send it barrelling sideways. A spray of gravel was spat from the right rear tyre as he fought for control, but we were through the turn and picking up speed once more as he straightened out and smashed the pedal again.

I relaxed my grip on the roof handle above my head and risked a glance in the door mirror.

'Are they still behind us?' Jagjit asked, his voice betraying his nervousness.

I peered into the mirror once more. The road behind us was clear but I could only see as far back as the corner we had just come around. I watched, counting seconds in my head. One, two, three... Then the huge black car shot into view, its blocky nose looking like a threat bearing down on us.

'Yup. And gaining fast.' I settled back into my chair, but I was hardly relaxed.

'There's no way we are going to make it,' Jagjit whined.

'Just keep going, mate.' I needed to keep him calm, keep his thoughts on the road. At the speed he was driving, it could all go wrong so quickly if he took his attention away from the next bend, the next obstacle.

We were on Drythorn road, heading out of Maidstone, doing over eighty miles per hour where the limit was fifty. It was anything but safe, but we had no option but to keep going. We had a long stretch of straight now, maybe a mile where he could push his speed.

I glanced over my shoulder at the car behind us, it was gaining. The driver less concerned for his safety than Jagjit. I saw Jagjit glance in his rear-view mirror also, then utter a loud expletive. I was thrown forward against the seatbelt as he slammed on the brakes.

Less than one hundred yards ahead of us, a tractor had pulled onto the road, emerging from a field with a loaded trailer on the back. Jagjit's tyres were skipping over the road surface, once again fighting for grip as he tried to avoid hitting the slow-moving object unexpectedly in front of him.

Quite how the black four by four behind us hadn't hit Jagjit's back end was beyond comprehension. There was no way Jagjit could slow down in time, our speed was too great.

The tractor though was driving with one enormous wheel against the hedgerow. The other was in the middle of the road and the gap to the hedgerow on the other side was maybe just big enough for us to slip through. Jagjit had seen it too.

'Dammit,' he swore as he flicked the steering wheel. With no choice but to try it, he lifted his foot from the brakes and, still doing forty miles per hour, he shot by the surprised farmer.

The driver's door mirror caught something solid in the hedge and smacked against the glass of his window, the sound loud in the quiet confines of his car. Then he was fishtailing back onto the road ahead of the tractor. I swung around to see if the larger black car would make it through.

'I think we lost them,' I told Jagjit.

His face grim, he didn't answer. He just pushed the pedal closer to the carpet and picked up speed again.

'We are going to make it, mate. Don't worry.'

He glanced across at me. He was sweating with worry.

'It's only a fitting,' I pointed out.

'Tempest, you would not believe the strings my father had to pull to get us an appointment here at all. When I enquired, they said they couldn't fit me in until March. I mean, March! I'm getting married in four weeks. So, when this cancellation popped up, I knew it was my only chance. What's the time?'

I shot my cuff to check my watch. '1723hrs.'

'Dammit.'

'We are going to make it. They said they would stay open as long as you got there before they close. You have seven minutes and it's only three or four minutes away.'

'They got through,' he announced excitedly.

I looked behind to see Big Ben's huge Ford Ranger bearing down on us again. In it were Big Ben, Hilary, and Basic. The four of us were to be Jagjit's groomsmen. I only found out this morning that he had proposed. He had only been dating the lady for a few weeks but apparently, that is all it took in their case.

After the battle with the Klowns, which seemed like a lifetime ago but was, in fact, only two weeks ago today, he had considered his options and popped the question. She had been present when they attacked and had been distraught when he sent her to safety so he could come back to fight the Klowns with Big Ben and me. It had been a dangerous situation and could have gone far less positively than it had.

Anyway, Jagjit and Alice fell into the category of whirlwind romance, and they had set a date of November the 26th and now had to get a lot done in a short space of time. Jagjit thought he already filled me in, but his email had never reached me in Cornwall. It was of no consequence now.

He had left work early today to organise his groomsmen, and we were at his parent's house chatting about what he needed us to do, where the wedding was going to be and a million other details when the call had come through to say Anton Ricoh, famed wedding outfitter, could see us. In a blind panic, we had dived into our cars to blast our way cross-country to Meopham where his boutique bordered the village green. I had heard of the man but knew nothing about him and would never consider spending the insane amounts he was going to charge.

I mused though that chances were most grooms just did as their bride instructed. I was curious to hear if his Indian parents, with their extended Indian family were happy about their youngest son marrying a Caucasian girl. I would not bring the subject up though, so would only find out if he volunteered the information. He had been married once before, a distant cousin that had been pushed into the arrangement as much as he had, I think.

It had lasted only a few months, but I got the impression he gave it an honest try. Now he was in love it seemed, and desperate to please the lady now firmly rooted at the centre of his life.

He slowed his pace as we came to Meopham village outskirts. It was not a big village, the green was directly ahead of us, so with four minutes to spare we were pulling up outside the double fronted shop.

Inside the windows were immaculate suits, hats, gowns, dinner jackets and wedding suits displayed on mannequins. In quite small gold writing it boasted that the proprietor served at the Queen's appointment.

The doors swished open, being held by two well-dressed young gentlemen and we were welcomed inside.

The Witches of East Malling:
Chapter Two

PUB O'CLOCK

Friday, November 4th 1917hrs

The fitting had eaten up only an hour. For the most part, it had been entertaining as the tailors had struggled with the dimensions of both Big Ben and Basic. I will admit the five of us look like a study in genetics when put in a line. Big Ben stands six feet and seven inches tall and has wide, muscular shoulders tapering to a thin waist because he's lean like a professional fitness model. I carry enough muscle to be called athletic and spend a reasonable amount of time in the gym, but I also have a covering of body fat masking my abs because unlike Big Ben, I cannot drink beer and maintain a perfect figure. Hilary is as skinny as a rake. No matter what he wears, he looks like it's two sizes too big and hanging from his bony frame. Jagjit is slight but is arguably the most generic or normal looking one of us and then there is Basic. Basic is blocky, Basic is above average height and Basic is wide. If a witch turned a fruit machine into a human and gave it flesh, then Basic is what it would look like. He was maybe a couple of inches taller than me, but one couldn't tell because he was permanently slouched. I estimated that he weighed fifty percent more than me and it was almost all muscle.

When the fitting was done, Jagjit had come away happy. The suits would be made up in time for the big ceremony in four weeks, so we had thanked the gentlemen and left them to close up. It was the first time I had been fitted for clothes since I left the Army. Back then, there were appointed tailors that provided ceremonial uniforms and did a great side business in hand-fitted suits.

The drive back to Finchampstead had been at a more leisurely pace, the panic of missing out on something thankfully gone. It was now Friday evening so, as practice dictates, it was time to frequent the local alehouse and sink a few cold beverages.

The village only had one pub, the Dirty Habit, so named for the Friary just outside the village to the south. Our visits there had become a regular Friday night event. Big Ben had ditched his car at my place, and I had hopped out of Jagjit's car next to an alleyway that connected where his parents lived with the street my house was on. I needed to go home and collect my dogs. The two pesky dachshunds were popular at the pub. There they would be given affection and attention by eighty percent of the patrons.

I pushed open my front door as the two dopey sausages tried to force their way out of the widening crack.

'Hey, chaps,' I greeted them as they climbed my legs for attention. I came down to their level so they could lick my hands as I scratched their ears and necks. 'Ready for a trip to the pub?' I asked as I took their collars and leads from the wicker basket I kept on a shelf next to the front door. They buzzed around my feet in excitement.

Whether they understood what I asked them I couldn't tell, but I knew they would drag me into the pub if I took them in that direction and they were generally happy to go out for a walk despite their natural inclination toward laziness.

No more than ten minutes later, having circumnavigated one half of the village in a circuitous route that exercised the dogs, I entered the pub car park with them both straining at their leads as they dragged me to the door and into the warm.

The alcohol-scented walls of the Dirty Habit were familiar and comforting. It was a place where I had spent many hours talking nonsense and drinking beer. To my left, an open fire was kicking out not only heat but the wonderful smell of a real fire. The accompanying crackling, popping noises a joy to hear. To my right, was a roundtable with the four chaps sitting around it, already halfway down their first drink as they hadn't wasted precious drinking time fetching their dogs as I had. Whoever had bought the first round had been thoughtful enough to get a pint in for me. It was sitting untouched in front of an empty chair, condensation running down it to wet the cardboard mat it was sitting on.

In front of me, was the bar. I had no reason to approach it as I already had a drink, but for the first time in a few weeks, Natasha was serving. Now that I thought about it, it was I that had been missing recently. The last two Fridays in a row I had been absent so she might have been here after all. Whether she had or not, it seemed like a long time since I had seen her.

I debated waving a hello in her direction. I wasn't sure what our current relationship status was though. About a month ago she had kissed me and placed the ball in my court. I was probably supposed to have used the ball to score a goal if that is not extending the analogy too far. Instead, I had lost the damned ball or in actuality, her number, so I hadn't called and by the time I tracked her down she had decided that I wasn't worth the effort. I worried that she might be right.

She noticed me standing near the pub entrance though and smiled in my direction. She had been quite short with me the last time we spoke, so this was a marked improvement. Buoyed by that, I smiled back at her, gave a little wave of greeting and took my seat.

'Evening, chaps. Did I miss anything?'

'Only Big Ben telling us about his latest shag. It seems he finally broke his once only rule,' said Hilary.

'And he thinks he might have got a girl pregnant,' added Jagjit.

'Oh? Occupational hazard I should think, Ben. We can circle back to that bit of information. I want to hear about Patience. How did that come about?' I snagged my pint from the table and gulped down a third of it in two swallows. It had started to warm already but was still pleasantly cold.

'It was mostly your fault,' Big Ben replied accusingly.

I set my pint down, my brow ruffled. 'I don't follow, dear boy. Do explain.'

'I ended up spending half of last week with Hotstuff. With you away, she was getting herself into bother. Did she tell you about the spiders and the snakes?'

'She did.'

'What about spiders and snakes?' Jagjit wanted to know.

'I'll tell you later, mate,' said Big Ben before turning his attention back to me. 'So, I rescued her from a gang of kids on the Magdalene Estate, then went with her to rescue a client that was being stalked by the voodoo priest dick and ended up staying at her place because the client said she felt safer with me around.'

I thought about it for a second, 'You mean you shagged her.'

'Well, obviously, but I prefer to think of it as *really* close protection. Anyway, that was Monday night and after that the whole week slipped by without me getting another shag.'

'I still don't see how that is my fault,' I stated, taking another sip of my drink.

'Because to start with, I figured that it was only fair to give you the time you needed to finally pluck up some gumption and give Amanda a seeing to. I know how much you like her. You have been a mooney-eyed kid since she turned up last month.'

I opened my mouth to protest, but around the table, all the others were nodding their agreement. I stayed silent.

Big Ben continued, 'Then I discover she has a boyfriend. Some rich butthole, but she let it slip that she hadn't got around to sleeping with him yet. So where does that leave me? She isn't interested in you because she's dating someone else, she isn't sleeping with her boyfriend because of goodness only knows what reason. So, I figure I might as well remove all the charm suppressors that have been stopping her from throwing herself at me, vagina first, like any sensible woman would, but having done so, nothing happened. I swear that girl is broken. I thought it might have been shark week, but then she stayed a night at my place when the spiders were rampaging hers and she didn't bring any feminine products with her, so it wasn't that either.'

He lapsed into silence. I gave him a minute.

'I still don't get it. What does Amanda's ability to see

what a scumbag you are, have to do with you sleeping with Patience for the second time?'

'Oh yeah. Lost track of what I was saying there a bit. So, Tuesday night no action because I'm with Amanda. Wednesday night no action because I'm with Amanda again but this time she's dressed as a man and all the girls stay away because they assume I'm gay. Thursday night I spent getting tortured and beaten. By the time today had rolled around I had gone three days without sex. When was the last time you went three days without sex?' he asked me, then indicated the question was open to the rest of the table.

'Right now, actually,' I replied.

'I'm married,' replied Hilary. When we looked at him to clarify his answer he said, 'I hardly ever have sex.'

Basic had no answer and Jagjit was grinning because he now had a girlfriend, and I was willing to bet they celebrated the sun going up and going down by visiting each other's private places.

'Weak. Just weak,' Big Ben said shaking his head. 'In contrast to you shandy-sniffing, lightweight excuses for men, I last went three days when I was fourteen. By last night I was starting to get the shakes.'

'You can't get the shakes from having no sex,' I replied.

'How would you know? You can't go cold turkey if you never get any turkey to start with. Patience offered me no-holes-barred action, and I took the deal.'

'Wait. The expression is no-holds-barred,' pointed out Hilary. 'It comes from wrestling where, in some bouts, there are certain holds that one cannot apply to an opponent ...' He saw our expressions and realised he'd misunderstood the premise.

Jagjit leaned over and whispered in his ear.

Big Ben grinned.

Hilary caught on. 'Oh,' he said quietly, his cheeks flushing.

'Anyone want to go to see the fireworks at Leeds Castle tomorrow night?' Big Ben wanted to know.

'Maybe. Let's get back to the bit about you getting a girl pregnant first though, shall we? How did you even find out? I thought you always sanitised their phones to remove your number before you left?'

'I do. Remember the Big Ben business cards?'

'Yeah. For all your vaginal needs. Isn't that the marketing strapline you use?'

'Yeah. Works like a charm,' he boasted, then remembered his plight and looked unhappy again. 'Well, I hadn't thought that thing all the way through and it had my number on it.'

'Making you easy to find.'

'Yeah.'

'Do you even remember her?' Hilary asked.

'Of course. I keep a journal. She was the super-hot redhead on September 9th. I met her in the coffee shop on Fremlin Walk.'

'You don't know her name, do you?' Jagjit said.

'It's Bethany,' he replied, exasperation creeping into his voice.

It was my turn to ask a question, 'Did you know her name before she told you what it was today?'

'Nope,' he said proudly. 'That's why she's listed as the super-hot redhead.' Just then his phone pinged. It often did that and usually, it was a woman looking for sex. He often left the pub on a Friday night with a woman waiting outside his apartment for him to get there. As he looked at the screen his expression changed from one of mild curiosity, wondering what the message might be, to one of dread. 'I don't believe it.'

He put the phone on the table face up so we could see it. Hilary, Jagjit and I all leaned in to read the screen. Basic leaned in as well, but I think he only did it because everyone else was. I wasn't sure if he could read.

'Hi Ben, It's Britney. I need to meet with you. I think I'm pregnant.'

'Oops,' said Hilary.

'They say problems come in threes …' Jagjit smirked.

Big Ben locked eyes with him. He wasn't seeing the funny side.

'Soooo. How about the fireworks then, buddy?' I interjected to break the tension.

'I'm going to the gents,' he announced, standing up.

'And I'm going to the bar.' I collected the empties as Big Ben wandered away. 'Same again all around?' I confirmed. There were nods in reply and a thumbs up from Basic.

At the bar was Natasha, waiting to serve me.

'Hello, Tempest. Are you well?' she asked as she took the empty glasses

'Yes, thank you, Natasha. Are we friends again?'

'Same drinks, yes?' she enquired, dealing with business first. She was dressed much the same as always with one of those miracle bras that made her ample breasts defy gravity and a top that showed off a surprising amount of them. Her hair was getting longer, her natural, lustrous brunette locks falling over one shoulder to hang lower than her boobs. She positioned two glasses to begin pouring drinks, then glanced back up at me. She had made me wait a few seconds before answering my question. 'That, I think, depends on whether you still think you deserve a second chance and what you might do with it if there was one.'

From below the bar, Mr Wriggly had grabbed a bugle and was calling reveille to his two small round friends.

I was flapping my lips and failing to speak as usual. Mr Wriggly was getting cross with me. If he had a foot, he would kick me in the two friends sitting just below him. It was an idle threat, but I put my brain into gear and formed a response anyway.

'Whether I deserve a second chance or not, is not for me to decide, but I will say that I feel we will both miss out if we do not pursue a second date.'

'A second date?'

'I'm counting lunch in Rochester as the first date. We were alone, it was nice, we kissed. It felt like a date to me.'

'Are you trying to get to date three, Tempest?' she asked, a single eyebrow raised.

My cheeks felt warm. 'That's not really how I do things, Natasha. I'm not looking for a date because I want a particular outcome. I would like to talk to you about what I do want if I can entice you into coming out for dinner with me.'

'Well, I don't know, Tempest. It might have to be something special if you want to *entice* me.' She was teasing me. She finished pouring my beverages.

'And take one for yourself,' I said as I handed over thirty pounds. 'When are you free?'

'How about Wednesday evening?'

'I'm always free, lady. If Wednesday works for you, then I will make dinner reservations and will pick you up.'

'Well, you have my number.'

'No, I don't actually. That was the problem. You wrote it on a note, and I don't know what I did with it, but I never saw it again. I'm not even sure I took it out of the restaurant with me after you handed it over.'

'Oh,' she said, her face colouring slightly. 'I thought that was just some excuse you came up with for not calling me.'

'No, I'm genuinely stupid. I lost your number and had no way of getting it. I don't even know your last name and the Landlord, bless him, is very protective of you. I near enough begged him for your number, and he wouldn't give it up.'

'Bless him.'

That's not what I had said.

From behind me came a fake coughing noise. The chaps wanted their drinks and were being dicks about waiting while I sorted out my life.

'You go,' Natasha said. 'You're drinking, so this is not the time to talk properly. I will look forward to Wednesday. First though, give me your phone.'

I handed it over and watched as she created a new contact called Natasha Stow. She saved it and now I really didn't have an excuse. I didn't feel that I needed one though. I was back on track with Natasha, a woman I had been interested in for a long time.

I left her with a final smile and went back to the chaps, trying very hard to not look like the winner I knew I was.

I had snagged a bag of pork scratchings for the dogs to share. Their Friday night treat. I would usually split it three ways and eat a third myself, but in contrast to their trim waistlines after a week of getting far more exercise than usual in Cornwall, my waistline had expanded, and I was topping it off with several beers now. I was going to start a whole new regime tomorrow. I had already stocked my fridge and cupboard with the food I needed to be eating. So, while I gave myself the concession of a Friday night drinking with the boys, I didn't want to add to that with deep-fried pig skin.

The dachshunds were climbing my legs to get to them anyway, so I upended the bag and watched them do a damned good impression of a Hungry Hippos game as they made the crispy treats disappear.

The chaps wanted to hear about my time in Cornwall. They had seen the news reports and the reporter I had met there was still covering it, her face being beamed around the world no doubt as the treasure was to be slowly excavated and catalogued.

I launched into a long-winded tale of my Cornish adventure and the beer flowed.

Something Jagjit and Hilary were talking about had caught Big Ben's attention. He and I had been talking about his pregnancy dilemma, then he wasn't listening because he was paying attention to them instead.

'What's going on?' I asked.

'I was telling Jagjit that he needs to establish dominance straight away when they move in together,' said Hilary. 'I didn't and have always been the one taking orders instead of giving them.' He looked miserable.

'Is that how you see it?' I wanted to know. 'Anthea rules over you? Shouldn't it be mutual with both of you as equals?' I had never been married but just as I couldn't imagine being subservient to a woman, I would equally have no wish to dominate her either. That didn't sound like any kind of partnership to me.

'That's how it is. I let Anthea make some decisions, gave her the accounts to manage, that sort of thing and she just kind of took over. Before I realised it, I was operating to her schedule, doing what she told me. Fifteen years in I don't see how I can change that.'

Big Ben was shaking his head. 'Mate, are you sure you don't suck balls for a living? Women like to be dominated.

Not in a manner that makes them feel diminished, but so they feel that you are their support, their strong arm to rely on, their big, manly man. Plus, in the bedroom, they all love to be dominated. Ever meet a lady that doesn't love to be spanked?'

'I've never tried,' admitted Hilary.

'There you go, mate. You could change the dynamic of your relationship with a little playful spanking. Pin that lady against the wall, give her a seeing to she won't forget, and she will want you to take the reins.'

'You have met my wife, right?' he asked.

Big Ben took a long swig of his drink and set it back on the table. 'All ladies are basically the same, buddy.' He claimed knowingly. 'Give it a try. What harm can it do?'

Hilary grabbed his glass while he thought about his answer. He opened his mouth to take a swig but stopped with the glass halfway to his lips. 'I don't know,' he concluded.

The group fell silent for a moment and when the conversation picked back up the topic had moved on to rugby and who was going to win this weekend.

Later, at home, I settled the dogs onto their side of the bed and slid under the duvet on my side. As I laid down to sleep, I thought about Natasha.

Grab your copy...
vinci-books.com/witches-eastmalling

About the Author

When Steve Higgs wrote his debut novel, *Paranormal Nonsense*, he was a captain in the British Army. He would like to pretend that he had one of those careers that must be blacked out and generally denied by the government, and that he has to change his name and move constantly because he is still on the watch list in several countries. In truth, though, he started out as a mechanic - not like Jason Statham in the film by that name, sneaking around as a hitman, but more like one of those sleazy guys who charges a fortune and keeps your car for a week even though the only thing you went in for was a squeaky door hinge.

At school, he was largely disinterested in all subjects except creative writing, for which he won his first prize at the age of ten. However, calling it the first prize he won suggests that there were other prizes, which is not the case. Awards may yet come, but in the meantime, he enjoys writing mystery and thriller novels and claims to have more than a hundred books forming a restless queue in his mind because they are desperate to be written.

Now retired from the military, he lives in southeast England with a duo of lazy sausage dogs. Surrounded by rolling hills, brooding castles, and vineyards, he doubts he'll ever leave, the beer is just too good.

Acknowledgments

I wish to take this brief opportunity to thank some of the people that allow these books to come into existence. First of all, and none too surprisingly I have to thank my wife for putting up with me disturbing her sleep as I roll out of bed all too early most mornings to start pounding the keyboard once again. I wish to also thank my two-year-old son for not drawing on my notes too often and for not accidentally pouring his milk into my laptop. There are others involved in this process because I cannot make the cover art by myself – I'm just not artistic enough, so thank you to Jacqueline Sweet, but most especially I wish to thank all the slightly odd people that believe the paranormal world exists. Without you I would have no fuel for the stories I write.